Demon Dog

to Mary –

Yo Yo wants you to enjoy Demon Dog.

Wick Hamilton

Demon Dog

Lori Hamilton

iUniverse LLC
Bloomington

DEMON DOG

This is a work of fiction. All of the characters, names, incidents, organizations, and dialogue in this novel are either the products of the author's imagination or are used fictitiously.

iUniverse books may be ordered through booksellers or by contacting:

iUniverse
1663 Liberty Drive
Bloomington, IN 47403
www.iuniverse.com
1-800-Authors (1-800-288-4677)

ISBN: 978-1-4917-0262-8 (sc)
ISBN: 978-1-4917-0261-1 (hc)
ISBN: 978-1-4917-0260-4 (e)

Library of Congress Control Number: 2013914078

Printed in the United States of America.

iUniverse rev. date: 12/06/2013

In memory of BoBo. For eighteen plus years, a perfect dog.

Acknowledgments

First and foremost to thank is Jean Jenkins, my editor. While she corrected, changed, improved and made worthy suggestions, she taught me about writing and what it takes to be a writer. I owe her so much.

A major contribution was made by Joe Shaw, managing editor at Cypress House Publishing Co. Although he rejected a very early and, admittedly, rough version of Demon Dog, he kindly edited every page with tutorials, and suggested he would be interested in a book about a dog that could speak.

Innumerable valuable additions came Ronnie O'Donnell, a fellow writer.

Encouragement came from those friends willing to read the first draft. To Cleo Balden and Gail and Michael Burton go gobs of gratitude. It took a real friend to plow through it at that point.

This book will be published specifically because Barbara Frier offered to read it, and then gave it to her husband, Chris, to read. Their review came in the form of a bottle of fine champagne to celebrate what they thought was a marvelous story that should be published.

Chapter One

Angela took a deep breath and walked into the bright lights of the television studio. The audience applauded as she took her place on the sofa. The host welcomed them with his signature lighthearted banter. Then he issued the challenge. "Okay, let's hear it."

Starting with something she knew he could say, Angela spoke to the furry bundle in her lap: "Say Maaa-maaa." She repeated, "Mama, maaa-maa." He listened, tilting his head from side to side as she spoke, pink tongue panting from the heat of the lights, but remained silent. Frustrated, she tried coaxing him. "Come on, darlin'—say maa—maa. You can do it."

The audience watched in anticipation as she bounced him on her lap. "Baby doll, you did it before. Just do it again. Please! See all these nice people waiting to hear you speak? You know, just like you do at home."

An incredulous Jay Leno asked, "He says it all the time at home?"

"Yes, he does. And he says other words too. Eat. Out. Play. Play is the hardest one because of the *p*. It requires puckering of the lips. Come on, darlin', pucker up those little lips." Angela showed him how to do it. She puckered and puffed out a *p*, making a soft "pooh" sound. It seemed feasible that he could duplicate her efforts, but Brandy was more interested in the audience—a sea of faces and lots of tantalizing scents. His lips didn't move, but his nose quivered with excitement.

Jay agreed. "Yeah, I imagine it would be a little tough for him to pucker." The audience snickered at such an improbability. "How did you ever get the crazy idea that your dog could talk?"

"Right. I thought it was crazy, too, when I heard Barbara Walters say her dog told her he loved her. Then I began to think about it. I started listening to all of Brandy's sounds."

Brandy was a tiny Yorkshire terrier, appropriately named because of his long, silky, black-and-gold coat. He was Angela's constant companion and sole roommate—her only diversion other than an occasional excursion to Las Vegas with her friend Agnes. The music of the slot machines was hypnotic, but the blackjack table was the magnet that pulled them back for more visits. If the pros at the table thought the two older ladies were easy targets, they soon learned that behind the bifocals and gray hair were minds that could count as fast as adding machines. In fact, Angela bought Brandy with her winnings from one session.

"Then I began daily sessions of repeating sounds over and over. At first he barked in response. But slowly I noticed the barks changing. I began to hear interesting sounds. Sounds like words. Not distinctly, of course, but a reasonable facsimile."

"How long have you been hearing *sounds?*"

The audience laughed at the implication, but Angela explained.

"Each time he tried, he got a cookie. His favorite animal crackers. Chicken-flavored. Before long, as soon as I took the box out of the pantry, he knew what was expected. It was like a game to him. We practice every day."

"If he talks every day, why won't he say something now? Let's hear 'eat, out, play.'"

"I think he's apprehensive. He doesn't know you. I think he needs to check you out. Here, you take him. Then he may talk for us."

She pushed the tiny dog over to Jay. He hesitated but then reached out to pick him up. An ominous *Grrrrrr … grrrrrr … grrrrrrr …* stopped him, and he quickly withdrew his hand.

"Hey, that's the same thing my dog says when someone tries to take his bone away. Does that mean that he's likely to start talking too?"

Angela was embarrassed. She hadn't expected Brandy to misbehave, especially not on national TV.

"I don't understand. He said several words when we were on the Letterman show."

Jay was gracious about it. "That's okay. Dave needs the ratings." Then he launched into a series of jokes that kept the audience laughing. Accustomed to a quiet neighborhood where the most activity on any given day was the postman dropping mail in the box or a rare visit from the UPS guy, Brandy reacted to the noise and jumped off Angela's lap. Barking as loud as a five-pound terrier could, he charged the audience right to the edge of the stage. His barks echoed throughout the studio.

"Yeah, boy, go for it," Jay cheered him on. "Now that's a conversation I can understand. He's telling us to get the hell out of here. Angela, you have a real winner here."

The audience applauded as Angela and Brandy made their exit.

Unseen by Jay and the audience, others had been watching the scene on stage. They nodded approval and made excited sounds. Copious notes were made on long, white scrolls.

Angela was discouraged but not defeated. In the taxi ride to the five-star hotel where the producers had booked her, she held Brandy close to her face and looked into his eyes.

Hugging him, she said, "Darlin', you disappointed me. But I still love you. As soon as we get home, we're going to work. You got some laaarr-nin' to do, honeybunch."

Brandy responded with his favorite word. "Eat." Or a reasonable facsimile. When he licked her nose, he tasted the makeup and coughed at the bitter taste.

"Ugh? Did you say 'ugh'?" My, my, how your vocabulary is increasing!"

Brandy has his own ideas about these efforts to help him communicate.

Do they think I was born yesterday? What comes after I learn to speak? Doing the dishes? Mopping the floor? Taking out the garbage? Is the next step putting a pencil in my paw and expecting me to write out *in cursive letters?*

No thanks. My "dog's life" is just fine, although I was confused when she started all the speaking stuff. I may not be able to produce those vowels and consonants she talks about, but I know we do communicate. She understands when I announce someone is at the door. I understand when she says, "Bad dog." Nevertheless, I will do my best and try hard to produce those vowels and consonants she wants to hear. I want nothing more than to please her. So I'll try. Really hard!

When they got home, Angela and Brandy continued their daily ritual of walks, play, bathing, brushing, and practice sessions. He curled up on her lap while she read or knitted scarves for the church to distribute to the needy.

One sunlit morning when they took their walk in the backyard, inspecting the garden for snails and weeds, Angela tripped over a tree stump. She fell to the ground, and when she couldn't get up, she thought her hip was broken. A trip to the emergency room confirmed her diagnosis. That's when Brandy's misfortunes began. The doctors told her she couldn't go home. Instead, they sent her to a convalescent home where complications developed. Complications that ended her life.

When Angela awoke, she was in a different place, a strange place. She looked around, but nothing seemed familiar.

Where am I? What kind of place is this? Well, I can see there's no dress code. I see lots of others in their hospital nighties too. It's kind of nice here. I'm actually floating. Never felt so free. I'd appreciate it more if I knew what's happening to Brandy. It's terrible for him to be left alone.

----Angela, you've been chosen.

Excuse me. I don't understand. What do you mean, "chosen"?

----We waited for the right person to arrive. We've been observing your work for some time. We believe you are the right person for our study.

What study is that, if you don't mind my asking?

----It's a study to determine whether Brandy has made actual progress in his ability to speak. Your work with him was encouraging and may prove that dogs are continuing to evolve according to the plan.

Oh, good! That means I get to go back to my dog.

----No. There is no going back. The law is that everything must continue to progress, expand. That is the law of the universe ... all universes. You cannot return to Brandy. If you accept this assignment, you will be trained for the mission. Then, after a brief tour of the

Dimension, you will be sent back, but as a spy. Only to observe and evaluate. And report to us.

Great! This is an opportunity to help my dog.

----You cannot help him or influence him. You can only report. If you are successful, you will be rewarded.

Rewarded?

----Yes. You will have two choices. You can choose to rise to the next level here.

But it's very nice here.

----Yes, it's hard to imagine that any place could be better. In fact, no imagination is capable of comprehending what the next level is like. It has to be experienced. It's the reward of rewards.

Or?

----The alternative reward is that you can make a wish, and your wish will be granted.

What happens if I fail with the mission?

----My dear, there is no punishment here. Only rewards. You will remain as you are now.

Okay! Then I'll do it. I accept. When do I start?

----Right now.

Chapter Two

I know darn well what Brandy would say if he knew I was back.

"I hate that you abandoned me."

It's true. I admit I did abandon him. It was unintentional, unexpected, and involuntary. But he doesn't know that, and, besides, he's not my dog anymore. I'm trying to deal with that fact as best I can … along with the shock of what happened to me. I still don't understand it, but I know I'm back with my dog. And that's a good thing.

Now he has a new name. YoYo. Can you believe such a silly name? Anyway, I'm hovering above his new home, waiting to observe him and begin my assignment. They said that I should try to get evidence that evolution has progressed enough so that *Canis familiaris* can talk. Well, at least manage a few words or a reasonable facsimile. This is of great interest to the Committee, whoever they are. They explained how they designed the process called "evolution." It's intended to improve the species—all species. They made it self-perpetuating so it doesn't require constant oversight. The Committee already has a full plate. But they say it's time for an evaluation to see how things are going with dogs.

I know there's some support on Earth where scientists agree that the dog's bark is the closest to human language of any animal sound. Since dogs have been best buddies with humans for at least a hundred thousand years, the prospects are reasonably good that communication can occur, especially considering the quality of the candidate they have chosen to study. The Committee chose YoYo over zillions of other candidates.

Unfortunately, when I was removed from YoYo, my son and daughter-in-law inherited him. That's when his life became hell. He was trained with a doggy door, but my son lives in a tenth-story condo. Both he and his wife work, so they left him alone all day. Need I say more about the numerous accidents, the messes to be cleaned up, my daughter-in-law's hostility, my son's anger, or the ignorant, abusive treatment they inflicted on YoYo?

When I passed on to the next world, they were relieved. They could get rid of him. Fortunately, they did the right thing and returned him to the breeder who sold him to me. That made him a rescue dog instead of a much-beloved, pampered pet who spent most of his days on my lap. The breeder took him back, knowing it would be hard to find a home for a mature male terrier, since most buyers prefer females. Because of the abuse, YoYo was shy and lacked confidence. But a miracle happened. A nice young lady came and took him home with her. She was very affectionate, and he fell madly in love with her.

I don't know whether he was in love with me. I only had him a short time. But I did love him dearly. I still love him. I want to pick him up and hug him, but I can't. However, I can encircle his little body, nestle in his soft fur, and peer into those black eyes. A big perk comes with this job. I get to be with the cutest little terrier in the whole world and watch his nonstop play. It doesn't matter that he can't see me.

He has a story to tell, and that's why he's a good candidate for our study. I know he remembers that he was born in a crib lined with newspaper. His mother seemed huge the first time he opened his eyes and saw her pink tummy. But then he weighed only a couple of ounces. Other puppies were feeding there too. He remembers how concerned his mother was when anyone picked up his brother or sister … and how one day some strangers came in, made lots of ooohhing and ahhhing sounds, and left with his sister. He and his brother missed her terribly. He remembers that soon after that, another stranger came, a lady with a cane. She held him the longest and then put him in a box and took him home. He cried all the way. But the next day, he found out how nice it was to be cuddled in a warm lap and soon adapted to his new mother. Me. The one who abandoned him.

What if he tells us about that abandonment? What he thought and felt, shedding some light on dogs' emotions ... What his life is like now with that new owner? I would give a lot to know whether he still misses me. I hope to learn all these answers.

This may be an impossible mission. Speaking is a problem for dogs because of their stiff lips and large, inflexible tongues. They do okay with some vowels—the yips, howls, barks, and growls. It's consonants that are the problem, especially p's. Imagine a dog saying, "Purple people pepper puppy." Their communication system works fine for them, but humans can't understand it, so we hope dogs can find a way to produce some words. Preferably in English. French or Chinese would present a greater challenge. I'm to look for key signs that speech is possible. Owners may be surprised, however, to discover how their dogs feel about those one-way orders: "Sit, stand, down, fetch, and roll over." And the possibility that dogs might issue a few commands of their own.

The breeder sold YoYo to a nice young lady whose name is Holly Hancock, for a mere $500. That's far less than the $2,500 I paid, the going price for a purebred Yorkshire terrier. Holly is a freelance writer specializing in educational issues. Some of her articles are published around the world. She lives in Los Angeles and is petite, with a wholesome, scrubbed look. Her dirty-blonde, shoulder-length hair frames delicate features, and she has big blue eyes. Needless to say, there's no resemblance to what I looked like.

I'm on duty in her house now and ready to use the helpful tools provided by the Committee. One of these tools enables me to know what's going on in the human mind. I was cautioned not to use this power indiscriminately and only to further the project. In other words, it's not a plaything. But I do wonder how humans would react if they knew we have access to all their secret thoughts. That would be a real game of "gotcha." Mention of what YoYo is thinking will be kept to a minimum in the report. We already know what he's thinking. If it's relevant, I'll include it in the report. It's what he's trying to say that is important.

Holly has worked all day and just looked at her watch. This will be my first chance to enter someone's head and see what's there. Here we go! Dare I say, "Whoopee"? As I tune in, she seems irritated about something.

Oh no. It's 5:40. Where did the day go? I forgot about that check from Brazil. It should be deposited, but I don't want to put it in the ATM. The bank closes at six, so I better get on my horse and get going. Where did I leave my purse? I hope the car keys are in it, because now I'm rushing.

It's only ten minutes to the bank. I'll grab YoYo and take him with me—he needs all the exposure he can get.

I wonder what she means by "needs exposure." Exposure to what, and why? I'm sure I'll find out.

And YoYo isn't cooperating. He's run to his cage. Now he's rolled over in a submissive position. The poor darling is frightened. He knows she wants to take him with her, but he doesn't want to go. He's afraid of being uprooted again. Holly lifts him out, but he is unhappy. I carefully move closer. I want to hear the sounds he is making.

They're typical doggie sounds, "Oh, oh, oh," except he is moving his whole mouth and jaw with each "oh." But the mouth and jaw don't need to move to make an *o*. That means he's trying something else, maybe a consonant. I'll make an uneducated guess that he's trying for an *n*. So it's not "Oh, oh, oh." They're heading for the garage, and he's saying, "No. No. No." Well, it's a good beginning.

Holly's other dog, a thirteen-year-old lab, rises slowly from his cushion on arthritic limbs. Not wanting to be left behind, he follows. There may be some sibling rivalry here. I hitch a ride on the roof of her car to rest my wings and save a little energy. It took quite a bit out of me to get here from the Dimension.

She pulls into the parking lot at 5:50, with ten minutes to spare, rolls down the window for the other dog, scoops up YoYo and her purse, and heads for the bank. The guard seems to know her, and Holly pauses for a moment to chat with him.

"Hey, that's some killer dog you got there."

"Hi, Joe. You may not be wrong about 'killer dog.' He's bitten my husband several times."

Now that's news to include in the report. What's that about?

"What's the problem?"

"It's only when anyone comes close to me. He's overly protective. He's a rescue dog. The trainer thinks he was abused. But he's also the sweetest little guy. I fell in love with him the moment I saw his picture. The way these little ears stand up in a big V are what got me."

She fondles YoYo's ears—the same thing I used to do when he was mine.

"What kind of person would abuse a cute little thing like that?"

Good question.

"The trainer says he needs to be socialized, exposure to lots of people and training. That's why I take him with me. You can pet him if you like."

None of this would have happened if I had been able to stick around. He didn't need to be "socialized" when I had him.

"Thanks, but I don't want to lose a hand."

They laugh as she enters the bank. It looks the same as almost every other bank, with a reception desk near the entrance, bank officials on the right and teller windows on the left. It's 5:48. The bank is almost empty, the usual greeter at reception is gone, and only two tellers are on duty. Holly joins two women in line. One is elderly and carries a shopping bag full of groceries. The other is a typical youngster, tattoos all over her body, a nose ring, another in, of all places, her exposed belly button. She has bright-orange hair with a turquoise streak. Tsk, tsk. She is pretty, though, and smiles at YoYo. Nestled in Holly's arms, he eyes her cautiously. The older woman reaches out to pet him, saying, "Aren't you adorable."

Round, unblinking eyes move to her. His little black nose twitches, pulling her scent into his nostrils. Scents are important and offer a wide range of information. What someone had for dinner last night, that a neighbor is barbecuing a steak or a raccoon was in the yard, or whether someone had sex. The human nose doesn't provide such information, which is probably a good thing. Imagine people sniffing each other. That would raise a lot of issues, and we'd need new etiquette to take the place of air kisses and shaking hands. Humans see their world. The dog smells his with an extraordinary nose.

Now YoYo turns his attention to a male customer at the teller's window. His nose is up, working its millions of efficient sensory receptors. That makes the dog nose superior to the human nose, which has a mere six million sensory receptors. Even more impressive is the beagle nose, with its three hundred million receptors. Proof that evolution has done a good job is that each one of the receptors in the dog nose has an army of tiny hairs to catch the chemical reactions that humans produce. Those include stress and fear. There is truth to the saying, "Don't let a dog smell fear." I don't know how many receptors a Yorkshire terrier has, but I can see that YoYo doesn't like the messages he's getting from the man.

It's now four minutes to closing time, and the second teller closes her station. The man at the window turns to glance at the women in line. When he frowns, his thick, black mustache turns down. Dark eyes are barely visible under his cap, and he glares at the dog. YoYo stares back, his nose still twitching. Holly instinctively pulls YoYo close and whispers to the other women.

"Maybe he doesn't like dogs." They nod in agreement.

The man turns back to the teller, puts his hands in the deep pockets of his jacket, and speaks in a low voice. I barely hear him, and I know we have a problem. But YoYo knew it first.

The tattooed girl puts her hand out to pet YoYo. Holly holds her breath, worried that a protective YoYo might snap. But the tiny nose just sniffs her hand.

"What's his name?" the girl asks. Both women laugh when they hear, "It's YoYo." Being friendly, Holly volunteers that they have another dog—a big, black Labrador named BoBo—and that he is in the car right now, waiting.

"When I got YoYo, BoBo wasn't thrilled to have competition. Then YoYo confiscated all the toys that BoBo had collected over thirteen years, including QuackQuack, a duck that quacks, and Ubba, a hot-pink teddy bear that cries 'Uuuubbba' when it's squeezed. But with this one"—she pats YoYo—"it wasn't long before QuackQuack didn't quack anymore and Ubba was silenced."

The women laugh again. Clutching her overloaded shopping bag, the older woman says she has mixed breeds that she got from the shelter. Holly watches the assistant manager walk to the front door, keys in hand. He waits for the guard to enter and locks the door. The bank is closed.

The man is still at the window. The teller stands motionless, with wide, unblinking eyes, listening to him.

"Money. Money. Give me all the money. *Now*. You too. *Now*." He points at the other teller.

"If you call the police, you won't leave here alive."

Both tellers step back from the window. The man's right hand comes out of his pocket. He's holding a 9mm semiautomatic Glock, which is pointed at the tellers. I'm totally unprepared for this. It could be bad. Reporting a bank robbery is not part of my duties. However, I was sent here to report everything about YoYo, so the study has to take a backseat. I watch the action from a sign that says Refinance No Points so I can record every moment of this drama. There is the possibility that these events might provoke YoYo. Maybe he'll erupt with a vocalization, a word. Two would be wonderful … more than we could expect.

Holly glances down at YoYo protectively. You have to love her because at this point, she is concerned about YoYo and what the man might do to him. The women in line gasp at the sight of the gun. He turns it on them and shouts, "Quiet! *Quiet!*"

Joe, the guard, moves toward the man, but the gun points at him, and he freezes. Joe and John Sanders, the assistant manager, can only watch helplessly. Waving the gun at the tellers, the man takes a large bag from a pocket.

"In here," he commands. To everyone else, he says, "Lay down on the floor. Now! *Now!*"

The older woman faints, drops her shopping bag, and its contents spill onto the floor. Holly reaches out, trying to grab her, and, in the process, drops YoYo. She kneels by the unconscious woman. The tattooed girl falls on her knees sobbing and then stretches out beside the woman. YoYo sits quietly until the man yells at Holly.

"I said, lay down on the floor now." He takes a menacing step toward her. There are no gray areas in YoYo's world. He explodes in a series of short, piercing barks, like rifle shots … *aawwffff … awwfff … aawwfff … aawwfff*. These are sounds typically used by dogs to provoke what's called "a flight response." I call it the formal warning. It may not be English, but the message it clear: *You'd better get the heck outta here. You don't want to tangle with me, buddy.*

Any intelligent person would understand that that bark is a warning. But not this guy. He chuckles.

"Yeah, perro, I am real 'fraid of you. You could eat me."

"Perro" responds by dashing to the man's pant leg and nipping it. Is this the same dog who slept so quietly on my lap for hours? I certainly never saw this side of him. Holly doesn't seem surprised. She knows this aggressiveness could be the result of abuse. But the man is amazed at the plucky, five-pound dog and laughs again.

"Perro, this is going to be fun."

Since when is robbing a bank "fun"?

YoYo grabs the man's pants and yanks. The man kicks at him, but YoYo is too fast and scoots in and bites the man's ankle. He is making some unusual sounds: *Heh … Heh … Heh … Heh … Heh … Heh.* His tongue hangs out, and his mouth is open. I am stumped, trying to translate those *Heh … Heh … Heh* sounds.

The man looks at his bleeding ankle and goes crazy, waving the Glock around.

"Enough with this dog. I want the money. I'm going to count to five. When I finish, you better have a bag full of money for me. One, two, three, four—*give me the money*—now! *Right now!*"

The teller takes the money out of the drawer and puts it in the bag, but she looks at the sparkling, new diamond ring on her trembling hand. She thinks about the date she has tonight with the man she loves to make plans for a fall wedding and fears she may not live to see him again. She hands the bag to the other teller who, without hesitation, puts the money in the bag and slides it to the man. As he reaches for it, YoYo strikes the other ankle, this time sinking his needlelike fangs into the bone.

"Aaaiiii!" the man cries.

Clearly hurting, the man jerks away from the bag and tries to grab YoYo, who is already ten feet away. The bag of cash tumbles to the floor. Nobody moves. The only sound is low-pitched and threatening, on a single note. Maybe a D-flat. YoYo's mouth is closed, his teeth are clenched, and his face is frozen except for the flaring nostrils. I can't see how he makes those sounds, but clearly, I hear a consonant needed to form a word—a G attached to the *u*, with an *a* in the middle. Another step forward, even if I can't translate *Guuuurrarrrrr ... Guuuurrarrrr* into English yet.

The older woman has regained consciousness. She props up on one elbow and blinks, trying to focus. The guard and the assistant manager lie prone on the floor. Both tellers are pale statues, except for the trembling of their bodies. The woman looks at them with sympathy. That desperate man will shoot them if the cops show up. He aims the gun at them, and she faints again.

Holly tries coaxing YoYo to her, but he remains where he is, eyes focused on the man. His nose wrinkles. Whiskers vibrate at a supersonic rate. The man grabs the bag of cash at his feet, now aiming at YoYo. Holly's heart pounds. She's afraid for YoYo but realizes that she can't stop his attacks when he's in protect-mode.

I know because I had the same experience. He even used to charge the vacuum cleaner and mop, making it hard for me to keep the house clean. They turned him into a ferocious animal. But that was nothing compared to the battle with the lawn mower. He hated the sound of it even more than the vacuum cleaner. As a matter of fact, he is supersensitive to all sounds—the doorbell, a car honking in the street. Sneeze, and he flies out of the room. A fart, and he dives under the bed. But he held fast with that lawn mower and rushed in front of it as it sped across the lawn. My gardener, José—that is, my former gardener, when I had a garden—was barely able to stop in time, just inches from that little body. Protecting me from that lawn mower was YoYo's job, and he did his best to kill it, even though he was scared. I could tell because his ears were back. That's the signal. Now it's his job to protect Holly, so the battle rages on in the bank, and his ears aren't back. I want to scream at the man, "Please, just take the money and go so this nightmare ends. So I can get back to linguistics."

As if on cue, the man grabs the bag and orders the manager to unlock the door. I wonder, *Did he hear me? Did I influence him? 'Cause that's a no-no.*

The moment the man approaches the reception desk, YoYo storms his ankles again and bites, barking a sharp, staccato series … *aawwfffffffff* … *aawwfffffffff* … *aawwfffffffff*, dramatically elongated, with lots of *f*'s. Consonants. Well, we're always glad to hear them, whatever the intended word is.

YoYo runs in circles, detouring to leap at the man's back. His jaws snap and tear fabric while the man runs toward the door. YoYo executes a flying leap at his knees—trips him. The man falls to the floor. The bag of cash slides under a desk.

The man crawls under the desk after the money. YoYo continues to circle at a furious speed, but now he's making the *Heh … Heh … Heh* sounds again. His mouth is open, his jaw is dropped, his cheeks are high. This is happening so fast. I struggle to record it. I never heard the *Heh … Heh … Heh* sound when I had him. He must have learned it at his new home. Oh, now I get it. It's a game. He runs in circles making those sounds. When he stops, Holly stomps her foot and that gets him running again. She calls it the Stomp Game. Not exactly Nintendo, but he likes it. But what does it mean now in the bank?

If I say "Hehhehhehheh" over and over, what does it sound like? It's "hahaha" or as close as he can get to laughing out loud! So "Stomp" is fun and so is taking the bad man down. Well, laughter is an important part of language. Birds can't do it. Snakes hiss, dolphins smile, and camels spit a good distance, but none of them can laugh. This is big.

But this time YoYo does stop because he sees an opportunity. A large derriere sticks out from under the desk. Like a projectile, YoYo leaps, jaws snapping. The bite must have hit a nerve somewhere in all that muscle and fat because the man screams, "Oooooowwwwww!"

The man forgets that he is under the desk and lunges at YoYo. His head collides with wood. We hear a loud thud. Blood trickles down his face. Stunned, he calculates the damage, glaring at the little monster guilty of inflicting these indignities.

YoYo sits up on his haunches like a meerkat, growling—*grrr, grrr, grrr, grrr, grrr, grrr, grrr*—deep, menacing sounds that pulsate and throb.

The robber pulls himself to a sitting position and leans against the desk. His face flushes almost as red as the blood smear. His legs stretch out on the floor. A defiant YoYo sits between his feet. Slowly and deliberately, the man raises the Glock and takes careful aim. It's a perfect shot. Except that the moment he fires, YoYo jumps toward him. Bull's-eye! The man missed YoYo and shot his own foot. His scream reverberates. He grabs the bag of cash with one hand, the Glock in the other, and stands. Screaming, "I'll catch you," he chases YoYo around the bank. "You're not normal. You're a devil."

He thinks cute little YoYo is the devil? Pardon me while I take a moment to have a good laugh here. Boy, is he in for a surprise.

Everyone holds their breath. What will happen next? Will he shoot YoYo? Will he turn the gun on them? No one dares to move except YoYo. He runs in circles and barks *Ggooofffchaaa … Ggooofffchaaa … Ggooofffchaaa.* Two syllables rapidly repeated over and over with *g*'s and *c*'s and the *f* again. "Gofcha"? This one's obvious. It doesn't take a stretch of the imagination to know he's telling Juan Carlos, "Gotcha! Gotcha!" What a guy! No, what a dog!

YoYo is so close to the floor and moves so fast that the man has to keep turning to aim his gun at him. Five turns later, YoYo's still racing around him. The man is dizzy, and bleeding. YoYo darts toward his ankles. Instinctively, the man squeezes the trigger. It's a mistake. He shoots his own foot—the other one. That's round three for YoYo. Screaming Santa Maria de la … the man sinks to the floor, overwhelmed with pain. Note: what followed St. Maria's name didn't sound very religious, so I left it blank. Anyway, the bad guy has been defeated. It's a knockout.

Squad cars finally arrive with flashing lights, sirens screaming. The bloodied robber rolls on the floor in pain, muttering, "Demon dog … demon dog."

One of the cops says, "What happened to you, fellow? You look kinda beat up."

You can say that again, and that's how I'm going to end the day's report, except that this is one of the few times I'll add YoYo's comment to wrap up the day's events.

Now can I have a cookie?

Chapter Three

Perched on a high ledge in the Hancock den, I diligently observe my former companion. This spot has a good view of the kitchen, the dogs' toy box, YoYo's cage, and the newly installed doggie door—important outposts for surveillance.

I watch YoYo play with a tiny rubber ball. He tosses it in the air and it bounces across the room. He dashes for it and makes those *Heh ... Heh ... Heh* sounds and tosses it again. This time it bounces high and onto the kitchen table, then off and into the dining room. It ends up under a cabinet. He crawls under the cabinet, retrieves the ball, and tosses it again. He only plays like this when nobody else is in the room. I am privileged to watch.

The other spying location I've chosen is on top of the speakers in the master bedroom, which doubles as Holly's office. This morning when her husband came into the room, YoYo snarled, barked, and then bit him. In fact, drew blood and left teeth marks on his calf. Ted was furious. The next time he came in, YoYo retreated under the bed. So he knew he had done a bad thing. I might add that when her husband did go back in, he brandished his robe like a toreador to prevent another attack.

The moment I saw Ted, I understood why YoYo attacks him. The mystery of why my dog morphs into a monster is solved: Ted is six foot two, with broad shoulders and long legs. That, along with similar features and coloring, makes him a dead ringer for my son—the one who punished YoYo. The one who rubbed his nose in the messes. The one who rolled up a paper and swatted him with it. Poor Holly. It's got to be a dilemma for her, and it makes me anxious. It would be terrible if YoYo had to go to a new home.

A detective called today. He asked Holly to go to the station and make a statement about the bank robbery. The incident generated a lot of attention. Dog Foils Bank Robbery was the headline in the *Los Angeles Times*. All the local stations ran with the story and showed pictures of YoYo, Holly, and a mug shot of the robber. Now the phone rings a lot with calls from the media who want to interview Holly and, of course, YoYo. She accepts all of them as opportunities to socialize YoYo and give him positive experiences with strangers that, with luck, will erase the effects of the abuse. So we've been busy, and it's been fun being in the limelight. Well, at least being perched on Holly's shoulder while she and YoYo are interviewed.

Friends came to the house last night to check on Holly, and YoYo charged them all. He didn't want to let them in and barked fiercely. However, after serious sniffs, most were approved and let into the house. Some had their hands licked. I'm sorry to say that the few who didn't pass the sniff test were nipped. But even they thought he was adorable.

Holly plans to take YoYo with her to the police station. Some of the officers want to see him. I'm kind of excited, because in my whole life, I had never been in a police station. This mission is certainly more interesting than any of us had anticipated. It's a reward in itself. Still, I should start thinking about the possibilities … make a wish or move upstairs. To the ultimate penthouse. Wonder if I get my own room.

I hitch a ride on the roof, but it's windy. Warm Santa Ana winds are blowing off the desert. I don't like it because my wings get battered, so I decide to move into the backseat with the big dog. At fifty miles per hour, it's difficult to slip through the window, and perhaps I am clumsy with my entrance, because now the big dog is aware of me, even though he can't see me.

His nose is in the air, trying to get a scent while his eyes scan the space I'm in. I hope he doesn't signal that there's an intruder. If YoYo becomes suspicious and senses that it's me, I've lost a big advantage in the study. Fortunately, BoBo now benignly gazes at my space as if he knows my mission is positive. Good dog. Just like a lab. I'd pat his head if I could.

We enter the station, and the cops give us a warm welcome. They call YoYo "hero dog," "partner," and "buddy" as if he is one of them. Officer Allen Bonner—he was at the bank yesterday—wants to hold YoYo. Holly reluctantly hands him over, but she doesn't have to worry. Officer Bonner doesn't look anything like my son, and YoYo likes him instantly, especially since he gets a belly rub. Officer Sam Weiner takes him, throws him in the air, catches him, and tells him he did a good job in the bank. Detective Clark Baker puts him on his lap, looks into his eyes, and says, "Well, little guy, I've got a really tough case. Since you're so good at catching criminals, maybe you can help me out." We all laughed at that.

I do like the way they talk to him. So many people don't bother, because they think dogs can't understand. What are words but symbols of things? Using words for symbols is the basis of language. Does anyone doubt that dogs know what "ball" is? It does get more complicated, of course, with grammar, and I still wait for YoYo to manage the tough consonants. Then we'll surely hear, "Ball, snacks, walk"—just some of the words he knows. In fact, one Border collie had a huge vocabulary and could identify two hundred objects after hearing the word, which proves that dogs do understand a lot of English. I'm not sure about other languages.

To reinforce my case, there is evidence that most animals know how to interpret the sounds that other animals make. As an example, when monkeys hear a leopard call, they run to the top of the nearest tree for safety so they can see it approach. Hearing an eagle cry, they run under a nearby bush or under the lowest branches of a tree for protection. When they hear a snake crawling through the bush, the troupe stands up in an open area and looks around on the ground.

Once I did an experiment to see whether my dog understood my words or read the signs I unconsciously gave him. From behind a closed door, I called out, "Do you want to go for a walk?" I said it in a monotone, careful that my voice didn't go up at the end, to indicate a question. When I opened the door, there he was, with the leash in his mouth, ready to go.

Taking this a step further, dogs respond to the *sound* of our voices too. High-pitched sounds are interesting, especially a meow. Sentences that end in question marks excite them. "Want to go out?" "Are you hungry?" or just plain "Ball?" trigger something close to ecstasy. They like giddy, happy sounds. Baby talk gets them to sit or stay faster than sharp, angry commands. It makes sense. Who wants to respond to someone who is angry and yelling, "Bad dog? Get over here!" A gentle "Come, good girl" usually works. A deep, low "No" can replace screaming, "Get out of the garbage."

Here's another point: tails talk. If YoYo holds his tail high, it's a signal that he is confident or that he's excited about something. When Holly first got him, his tail was down a lot because he was depressed, anxious, and stressed out. Now, that stub occasionally still curls under his tail and between his legs, but that's usually when he's scared. Especially after he's been scolded. He also tucks it under and rolls on his back when he's being submissive. What all dogs like to do with their tails is hold them really high so that their whole rear end is exposed. That allows their signature odor to escape into the air. It's the unique fragrance that invites, "Smell me, and know who I am." Sniffing tails is an activity they love. It's their version of reading a résumé.

I've also observed that dogs don't just wag their tails. They communicate with them. BoBo and YoYo usually greet Holly with tails that wag to the right. For a stranger, or a new dog, they tenuously wag to the left. When they play or search for a ball, it's a frisky tail that wags side to side, back and forth, or in big circles. My favorite is the "happy wag." That's when both BoBo and YoYo hold their tails high and race them. YoYo's shorty is a speeding pendulum, and BoBo's long tail is a fast flapper. My guests learned to hang on to their glasses when BoBo greeted them during happy hour. I call those wags "wiggles for giggles." I've made videos of dogs in parks and watch them play in slow motion to study how dogs use tail wagging for expression and communication. We shouldn't underestimate unspoken messages. We use them too. One type in particular is called writing.

In the police station, a big, powerful man watches the officers playing with YoYo from his office. He has a look of displeased disdain on his face, and he frowns when Officer Bonner rubs YoYo's belly. He is a tough guy and runs a large, no-nonsense division. A quick survey of his credentials reveals twenty-two years on the force, during which time he dedicated himself to pursuing criminals. He was good at it too—put a lot of them behind bars and earned the promotion that made him captain. Sad to say, from the dirty looks he sends Detective Baker, who is still rubbing YoYo's belly, he doesn't like dogs.

Although it's not relevant to this report, I suggest this information be forwarded for the captain's eventual evaluation by the Committee. I don't know if bad attitude lowers the chance for entry. But I do know that dogs are held in great esteem in the Dimension because of their fine, elusive qualities that humans quest for but can't seem to achieve. I'm referring, of course, to their ability to love consistently and unconditionally. Can you imagine a dog saying, "I don't love you anymore," if you don't give him that snack he wants?

The captain walks into the room and comments sarcastically, "So this is Wonder Dog?" But he thinks, *They act like wusses to fuss over a silly little dog.*

Please note that the captain did not actually say "wusses." I used discretion and did a substitution here, as per instructions to omit certain words. We know that cops have a varied vocabulary, even if they have to be politically correct when they talk.

The captain looks at YoYo with a raised eyebrow. A thought occurs to him. He is running for district attorney in the next election.

This little mutt might be a way for me to gain in popularity and win. Everyone loves a good dog story, and, hey, the dog is cute. Why not use it?

He watches as Holly finishes her statement, and she and YoYo leave. Then it hits him.

I'll give the mutt a special award. That's it. I'll hang some kind of a medal on it ... at a ceremony that will attract the media. The whole town will be involved.

He calls the public relations department, and they're excited about the idea. It's forwarded to the police commissioner. I'll bet my quota of new feathers that he goes for it. Why not? It's an opportunity to put a warm face on the department and improve community relations—a win-

win situation. A bubbly public relations gal is already on the phone with the bank president, asking whether the bank would like to participate in a special celebration to honor YoYo. She texts the news to Captain MacDonald: It's a go.

I can hardly wait. This event will give YoYo lots of opportunities to express himself, and I'll be there to record his take on it. The Committee will be eager to see that report, and, I hope, I'll gain some points.

Uh-oh. Speaking of the Committee, a warning arrives from them that I have used up my allotment of vices. We're allowed two. Previously, I bet my spare wing and now my quota of new feathers. It's a good thing for me that they don't demand perfection. I know gambling is a vice, but I thought I could edit this commentary. I didn't realize that it's monitored. Now I'm on probation and could be recalled. I don't want to be taken from YoYo again, especially before I finish the project. I must be more careful about my words, if for no reason other than to set a good example for YoYo.

Chapter Four

Supercautious about my expressions, I continue to study YoYo's sounds and activities. Mostly I watch for any tongue activity. A movable tongue is one of the prime reasons humans can speak. We're used to dogs panting with their tongues going in and out, but what I'm looking for is some sign that YoYo can wiggle his from side to side, as humans can. It's a short step from licking his chops, which he does as soon as a treat package appears. I'd be encouraged if that morphed into even a little side-to-side wiggle. It may be easier for him with his tiny tongue as opposed to, say, that of a St. Bernard.

The other important tool for speech is the larynx. Most humans don't know what a larynx is. They don't even know where it is, or that it's the airway, low in the throat, that lets them breathe. If we go back thousands of years, before language developed, we find humans with high larynxes. Today, they're still born that way, but at the age of three months, the larynx descends, making speech possible. That's precisely when a baby begins to vocalize, starting with "Mama." It happens again in boys when they hit thirteen. That's when their part in the chorus changes from soprano to baritone.

The success of the evolution of this one part of the anatomy allowed humans to communicate with understandable sounds, and those first, primitive sounds gave them an advantage in surviving. They made it possible for an early Paul Revere to grunt out some version of "The dinosaurs are coming! The dinosaurs are coming!"

Gradually those sounds ripened into the complex language we use today. Human language has come a long way, but it still needs substantial development before it reaches the levels of communication we use in the Dimension. A couple hundred thousand years might get people close. In the meantime, I'm looking for signs that evolution did the job, and YoYo has a lower larynx, so he can wiggle his tongue. Puckering his lips would help too. There is a good chance it's happening right now as YoYo chews on Ted's sock. My success depends on it.

However, even though the placement of the larynx makes speech difficult for dogs, I must admit that it offers them some amazing advantages—like breathing through their nostrils at the same time that they drink or eat. That means they can bark through their throat and whine through their nose simultaneously. I found that out in a shopping mall parking lot. Barks and piteous whines were coming from a car. *Two dogs in a car*, I thought. When I investigated, both sounds were coming from a Boston terrier—at the same time. That's awesome. Humans can't do that. It would be the equivalent of a human blowing his or her nose and drinking water at the same time

Even with their still-high larynx, dogs have been able to evolve beyond their wolf ancestors, who rarely use the bark to communicate and then it's a Johnny-one-note—a *wuuf*—to convey alarm. That means, "Pay attention. Something is going down." Wolves howl when separated from the group, at a family reunion, or the start of a hunt. "*Ouwwwwoooo*" translates to, "Let's roll." Dogs use a lot of variations of the "woof." YoYo has one he uses to get attention, and another—the *aawwfffff*—that's a warning. That's the one he used in the bank. The play bark is a rapid series of high-pitched *aarrffff … aarrffff*s accompanied by a happy expression and raised eyebrows. Yes, dogs do have expressive faces. That same bark, with wide eyes and active nose, is a good, old-fashioned "hello." Strangers get sharper, low-pitched *aaffffff*s designed to be heard at a distance. We'll get to the *rrruuuff*s and *hhhuuff*s later.

We also see progress in the way dogs have learned to vary the volume of their barks, which can be soft and gentle or go to an ear-blasting 130 decibels, depending on the content of the message. That means that while dogs waited to be able to speak, they figured out that volume and pitch can also be used to communicate. The most serious sound in their repertoire is the low-pitched *grrrrrr*. It figures. A high-pitched *grrrrrr* wouldn't scare anybody.

Because of domestication, dogs learned to use the bark to communicate with humans, and their first communication was probably to alert them to danger. The dogs chosen to be part of the family thousands of years ago became the first "watch dogs." Today, the bark is still an effective warning. With all that practice, they surely tried a word or two along the way. As the bonds between humans and dogs grew stronger, we believe that the gap between speech and the bark narrowed. Now they're considered members of the human family and undoubtedly want to get their two cents in.

BoBo and YoYo are definitely family. They spend all their time with Holly at home, where she works, and she takes them with her on errands—the market, the post office, the bank. She even took YoYo into a restaurant for lunch, tucked inside a large tote. I tag along and, although I am working, I'm having the time of my life. Oops. The truth is, I have more fun now that I ever did when I was alive.

Around the city we notice the banners that announce the celebration to honor YoYo. I look forward to it because it's been rather quiet at home. That is, except when YoYo bugs Holly while she's working. He keeps up the *mmmuuufff … mmmuuufff*s that grow into the irritating *arf … arf … arf*s. I understand his impatience. He's trying to have a conversation with her. *How about picking me up? Wouldn't you like a warm puppy on your lap?* And she's saying, "Be quiet, YoYo." To get some peace, she finally picks him up, although it's a snug fit at the desk for the two of them. Then she can go back to the piece she's writing about guns in schools. She decided to write about the subject because now she knows firsthand what facing a Glock is like. Her article argues that no child should ever be faced with that.

Her desk isn't really a desk. It consists of a piece of glass set on a Queen Anne table that holds a laptop, printer, telephone, and an old-fashioned rolodex. Strewn about on the floor are notes on scraps of paper, manuscripts, books, magazines, and files. Ted is also a writer who works from their house. His office is large, with a huge, green-lacquered desk, computers, telephone, printers, and the file cabinets he needs to do research for his historical novels that sometimes get on best-seller lists. The couple loves to travel, but now they are restricted. Plans for a safari in Africa or a Mediterranean cruise are deferred. They are reluctant to leave YoYo and BoBo in a kennel.

The big day finally arrives, and Julie is here to bathe and groom YoYo. She trims the long, golden, center-parted fall on his head that continues through his luxuriant, thick, black coat to his docked tail. Even though BoBo's daily swims in the pool keep him clean, he, too, gets a bath and some conditioner. Now his black coat is sleek and shiny. BoBo is smart and knows most of his toys by name. Ask him for "cushion," and he brings you a tiny pillow that squeaks. "Turtle?" gets you a beat-up, stuffed green toy. "Ball," and he dives into the bottom of the toy box where the tennis ball always ends up. That ball is of no interest to YoYo until BoBo plays with it. Then the focus is to get it away from BoBo. His persistence usually pays off, too, because BoBo, like most Labs, is not as aggressive as a terrier. Both dogs get spritzed with Armani dog cologne. Their reward for good behavior is one-calorie popcorn. I always loved popcorn and wanted to try some. Even if I could taste, I could never eat it without salt and butter. So I'll just leave it for BoBo and YoYo.

Holly announces, "Those Police Academy grounds are going to be windy." Her hair goes into a ponytail. Because it's a special occasion, she deviates from her daily uniform of jeans and a T-shirt and wears a red, pleated skirt with a new, white silk blouse and black sandals with five-inch heels. As she totters unsteadily to the garage, she says, "Wait a minute," and runs back to switch to practical red flats. Ted wears a pair of clean Dockers and a dress shirt. I have spruced up a bit too. Wings had a good fluffing up. Now they pile into the SUV, headed for the ceremony. I sneak into the back compartment before Ted closes the hatch.

A huge crowd is already there. We barely find a parking place. Food vendors do a brisk business, and the bank's big banners printed with We Love YoYo flutter in the wind. The grandstand is filled to capacity. Classes from the middle-grade school are in the bleachers, and kindergarten classes sit on the lawn, along with many parents. Bank employees hand out T-shirts to the children that are printed with YoYo's photograph and the bank's logo. The kids squeal with delight and pull them on.

Now they spot us mounting the platform, and a wild cheer—
"YoYoYoYo"—goes up. Ted and Holly laugh. I do too. Even BoBo wags
his tail, but YoYo is upset and squirms in Holly's arms. His ears rotate
like a radar dish. He wants to protect her from those strange noises,
including many that are undetectable to humans. The click of traffic
lights changing, all kinds of ultrasonic sounds, a siren in the distance,
a mother in the audience scolding her children—all those sounds flow
into his little ears. It's confusing, to say the least. He is used to familiar
background noises at home, like the hum of the fluorescent bulb, the tick
of a clock, a rat gnawing in the wall, or a cat tiptoeing through the yard—
all of which he barks at. He wants to alert Holly about the impending
threat, but it mostly annoys her because she doesn't hear those sounds.
What I don't understand is why it's so hard for him to switch from the
arf to announce, "Rat." The way I see it, the difference is just one letter
away from a word.

Holly also fails to recognize the variety in his barks that signals
the level of the threat. I'll translate: If it's a halfhearted warning—just
a couple of *wufs*—danger is not imminent. Someone walked in front
of the house or a car went by. A loud barrage means a squirrel had the
audacity to invade our territory. It's "Call Out the Marines" serious, or
his version of a 911 call.

The family takes its seats while I flop on a large YoYo sign. It gives
me a good view of the platform and the spectators. While Holly tries to
calm YoYo, she reminisces about how all this started. It's a good story,
so I'll include it in this report.

*All of this began six years ago, the day I married Ted. We had so much
fun together. We laughed at each other's jokes, teased, and bantered. When
he called on the telephone, the first thing I heard was him singing "I just called
to say I love you, I just called to say I care." He still sings every morning when
I get up—Here comes Miss America. BoBo fell for Ted too. Pretty soon it
became obvious that he preferred Ted, because he stayed with him in his office
all day, and they took siestas together and shared long walks. Oh, he was still
loyal to me—I knew he loved me, but as primary caretaker, I should have had
preference. In other words, I miss being number one with him.*

Ted reciprocated BoBo's affection. In fact, he liked to tease that he married me to get BoBo. I did tell him that we were a package deal. I was grateful that they bonded, because I'd known of cases where a new husband resented the wife's dog, and the dog suffered. Was even exiled to the backyard. But after a while, I began to feel like I wanted to have a dog of my own again. That's when I heard the radio station advertise an auction of thirty Yorkshire terriers at the local animal shelter.

News anchors and talk shows spread the news about these thirty Yorkies. They were all who had survived out of the hundreds shipped in boxes from a South Korean puppy farm. It's a good thing that customs officials confiscated the shipment of suffering, dying puppies and rushed them to the vet. Those thirty survivors had to be treated for six months until they were finally ready for adoption. I wasn't sure what a Yorkshire terrier looked like, so I went online. That's when I knew I was going to that auction at eight the next morning.

What high expectations I had, and how disappointed I was when I got there at 7:00 a.m. A double line snaked around the building and down the block. My $200 bid didn't win because someone bid $5,000 for a one-and-a-half-pound cutie held by a staff member who patted and rocked it like it was a crying baby who needed comforting. All the bids were in the thousands, so I gave up and went home. But I didn't give up entirely. I started a search, Googling reputable breeders whose prices fit my pocketbook, and spent hours calling, asking questions and learning about Yorkies. Then I received a photo via e-mail of a year-old male. I didn't want a male. I wanted a female. But when I saw that sweet, adorable face, the way those big ears on the little head looked like butterfly wings, my heart went out to him, and gender didn't matter. The breeder said the owner returned him because she got sick, making him a rescue dog, available at an affordable price.

But I still had reservations. I remembered my demotion to second place, and asked whether he liked women. She assured me that most Yorkies prefer women, and this little guy was very sweet. Sweet is right, but I had no idea I would get such a fearless protector, willing to attack anyone, including Ted and BoBo, who came near me. I wonder about that former owner. Why did she return him? Is he so defensive because she abused him?

My dear Holly, how I wish I could tell you what happened. Life was good for us until that day I tripped in the garden. I couldn't move, so I screamed my head off, but no one came. YoYo was really upset and tried to help me. He barked nonstop for hours until a neighbor finally came and called an ambulance. When they took me out on a stretcher, I cried and cried. I didn't want to leave him, and he wanted to come with me. They shooed him back in the yard, so he attacked them, bit several, and I could still hear him howling after the ambulance turned the corner. My son and his wife came to get him, but YoYo wasn't happy to see them. He didn't like my son. He'd heard him says things to me like, "What's that dog doing on the sofa," and "You shouldn't have a dog, in your condition." They took him back to their house but he refused to eat. Eventually, he had to eat, and that started the problems. The problems that, by the grace of the Celestials, led him to you, Holly. Although contact with humans is forbidden, I am tempted to touch your aura lightly with the tip of my wing. That should reassure you that it has worked out for YoYo. Sometimes rules need to be broken.

For a while I was afraid that I, too, would have to give him up if my marriage was threatened. But now I see Ted smile at YoYo as if he is proud of him. That means it's working out. Thank God.

We are surrounded by the mayor, the police commissioner, most of the city council, and that conniving captain from the station. The members of the high school band, resplendent in their uniforms, play the lively South Rampart Street Parade piece. It sets the mood for the event until police officers march onto the field. Now the band switches to another piece with lots of drums and trumpets. Officers line up on each side of the platform. In place, they salute YoYo. The officer who was at the bank, Allen Bonner, winks at us. The children cheer, and the adults applaud. The mayor, Emelio Santos, stands and walks to the podium. My goodness, how he loves being in the limelight. He is handsome, quite debonair in an elegant suit, probably Brioni, and welcomes everyone to the festivities. This crowd is upbeat, and they respond with applause.

"Ladies and gentlemen. Distinguished guests. Children. We are here today to honor someone special. That someone is here, and he happens to be a tiny, year-old Yorkshire terrier."

The crowd erupts into applause again, and the children chant, "YoYoYoYoYo."

"We know that dogs play a big part in all of our lives. I know that Samson, my collie, is my best friend. I'll bet most of you feel the same way about your dog."

I see the mayor is good at this, getting people to warm up to him. A necessary quality for politicians. He'll probably run for governor.

"I think we can agree that there is no greater task a dog can perform than to protect its owner. Today we welcome and honor little YoYo."

He turns to Holly.

"Please bring him here, Mrs. Hancock, so we can see a real hero."

Holly approaches the mayor with YoYo cradled in her arms, trying to keep him calm. I swing down from the sign and land on her shoulder. Holly holds him up for everyone to see. The sun filters through the center part of his golden topknot. The audience roars, and those tiny ears go straight up into a big V. Small black eyes survey the crowd. His nose wiggles to interpret all the scents that bombard his nostrils. He looks at Holly, tilting his head as if asking, "What's going on?"

She whispers in his ear, "They love you, baby YoYo. They think you're a hero … and you are."

Of all things, YoYo turns and gives her nose a big lick with a little tongue. The audience laughs, and he licks it again. Her nose is a frequent target, a source of fascination. Holly says he's giving her kisses. That's the way a lot of people interpret it, although those licks are a turnoff for others. Scientists say the dog isn't "kissing" and point out that pups lick until the mother regurgitates food, although wolves do greet each other with face licks. One thing everyone can agree on is that humans must taste good, or dogs wouldn't lick them. For me, an enthusiastic kiss-lick from my dog always felt like affection. So if it tastes good to him and makes me feel loved, how bad can that be?

Now Holly sets him on the enclosed glass stand prepared for him and moves to a nearby chair. He turns a couple of times and scratches his back before he sits down. Those little ears are straight up. He's agitated. His mouth opens, and his tongue moves, hopefully, from side to side. I encourage him because I think he's trying to say something. Keep trying, YoYo. Keep trying.

There's an *f*. Then a "whee" as he lifts a back leg to do some serious scratching. *Fwhee?* A reasonable facsimile to identify the problem—one of the most ignominious afflictions a dog can have. Their complaint is justified: *Why do we get them, and you don't?* Holly takes note. Tomorrow the bath will be with flea soap.

The mayor proceeds to tell the story. "This little dog, you see how tiny he is?"

He points at YoYo who, relieved of the itch, quickly stands in response. He stares at the mayor—erect, motionless—signs that he's ready to engage. A vibrating wet nose is like a magnet that grabs the mayor's scents and vacuums them in, scanning him about as thoroughly as any airport screener.

Again, the mayor points at YoYo. That makes the nose twitching accelerate. The audience roars its approval, but the police captain fidgets impatiently in his front row seat with the other honored guests. What's going on with him? Now he's complaining.

The way the mayor tells the story, he hogs the whole show. This is supposed to be my show. It was my idea, my plan to use this publicity for my benefit to win the election. By the time I present my medal, it will be anticlimactic. I should have known. I'm nothing but a dumb flatfoot, outsmarted by a shrewd politician.

Sorry, Captain, but you get no sympathy from me. You want to use a little dog in your scheme because you yearn to enter the arena of politics ... and you've got the nerve to complain about the mayor? Can't help but think of that saying, "What's good for the goose is good for the gander." I have a sneaking suspicion that the Committee will have the last word in the outcome, whatever that is. But then, they always do. I'm sure the deck is stacked in their favor.

"Is YoYo going to let that robber get away with the money?" The mayor builds the drama. "*I don't think so.* He runs in circles around the robber at warp speed—that is, Yorkie speed. Blood drips down the man's face, and he's in pain. He follows YoYo's movements and aims his 9mm semiautomatic Glock at YoYo."

The mayor has a good time with this, and he acts it out. He moves in circles with an imaginary gun in his hand as if following YoYo.

"But YoYo detours and dashes to his ankle for another bite. This time, right down to the bone. The gun fires. *Bang! Ouch! He shot himself in the other foot."*

The audience erupts in cheers, yells, and applause that last a full minute before he can continue.

"When our police officers entered the bank, they found a bloodied criminal cowering on the floor. He begged to go to jail. We owe a lot to this little fellow. We don't know what could have happened without YoYo—one of our citizens hurt, someone shot, the bank could have lost a lot of money. But he was there, and he did the job—for all of us."

Holly and I worry about YoYo. He watches the mayor, not taking his eyes off him, and we hear faint grumbles. Lips are pulled back with teeth bared. The mayor picks up a bright-red velvet box from the podium. The band does a soft drumroll.

"YoYo, on behalf of all the law-abiding citizens of Los Angeles, I want to present you with the first Medal of Canine Bravery."

He opens the box and takes out a shiny gold medal the size of a half-dollar, strung on a red satin ribbon, and reads the engraved inscription.

"The City of Los Angeles honors YoYo for the courage, determination, and bravery he exhibited on May 5, 2011."

I hear the captain sigh loudly. I know what he's thinking.

Hey, I'm supposed to bestow the medal. I hope the bank doesn't plan on giving one too. That would make mine just one of three. Da … [word sub], Darn it! I don't get it. Why do they make such a fuss over one little bank robbery? We would have caught the guy. We have the best department in the state. The getaway car was a stolen Lexus. A white stolen Lexus. How dumb can you get? He left his four-year-old kid in the car, packed and ready to head for Mexico while he held up the bank. His ex-wife says he kidnapped the boy. We coordinate with Border Patrol, and he's as good as picked up. So I don't get it, except that everyone is trying to cash in on this. I thought of it first. It was my idea, and it's supposed to be my show. "This isn't over yet," he mumbles to himself. "I'll think of something."

We'll see, Captain. We'll see, but I have a feeling that you're in for a big surprise before this report ends.

On cue, the drums roll, and trumpets blare. The mayor, prepared to award the medal, turns to YoYo. His eyes shift to Holly, questioning, and back to YoYo. She wants to warn him, "His nose is wrinkled. Don't try to put that medal on him." But before she can get a word out, the mayor reaches over, scoops YoYo up, and slides the ribbon over his head. Then he holds him up for all to see.

Darn, this guy is good. He was so fast that YoYo didn't know what happened until the mayor had him. The children scream with delight, everyone applauds, and Holly sighs with relief. Me too. It would have been a disaster if YoYo had bitten the mayor. What's that? Even the captain is thinking, *You have to give it to the guy.*

You don't have to give the mayor anything. He'll take it.

The mayor settles YoYo on his stand and begins introducing the president of the Bank of Freedom. YoYo immediately goes to work, tugging at the ribbon and gnawing on the medal. His objection? *I don't wear bling.*

"Stephen Mitchell always participates in our efforts to improve our city, to help its citizens, and provide efficient banking services. We welcome him to join us in honoring YoYo for the bravery he displayed at the Bank of Freedom ... Mr. Mitchell."

He could be typecast as the president of any bank—gray hair, tall and distinguished. The bank employees proudly watch him stride with authority to the podium. He clears his throat. It's as loud and important as I ever heard a throat cleared.

"Uhhhummm!" he utters. A commanding "Uhhhhhuuum." Whatever it is—star appeal, qualities of leadership, authority, or just plain confidence—this man has it. Everyone settles down, and he gets their attention.

"In my thirty-five years in banking, I have never heard of anything like the story of YoYo happening in our bank. I never heard of such an event at any of our branches. In fact, I never heard anything like this happening in *any bank, anywhere.* This little dog ..."

Oh my. He vehemently points his finger at YoYo, who interprets the gesture as aggressive and jumps up at attention.

"... deserves all the credit we can give him. And 'credit' means if he wants to buy a new doghouse for himself and his friend, he is welcome to come see me at the bank. You can be sure I'll make him a very good loan."

The audience chuckles.

"Our mortgage rates are the lowest in town. We're the friendliest bank."

He moves his hand to pet YoYo, but the already suspicious dog responds with his top-of-the-line bark—a holdover from his wolf ancestors ... *wooofffff ... woooofffff ... wooofffffff*. It's at least 130 decibels, with a high kilohertz frequency. Mr. Mitchell moves his hand to safety. An embarrassed Holly tries to quiet YoYo, but he turns the bark into a howl. *Woooooofffffoo ... woooooofffffffooo*. In the grandstand, a couple exchanges looks and a smirk. An incurable snoop, I drop in to eavesdrop on them.

"Yeah, YoYo knows the kind of loan he'll give him ... the same one he talked us into when we refinanced."

It seems that the loan had a lot of fine print, and they ended up paying a high interest rate. Maybe YoYo doesn't actually know this, but the nose that detects chemicals tells him to be on guard.

Holly pats YoYo until he settles down. Mr. Mitchell reaches into his breast pocket, removes an envelope, opens it, and takes out a check.

"The Bank of Freedom donates this check for $5,000 to a charity of your choice, YoYo. It's our expression of thanks. You not only protected your mistress, you stopped the robbery."

He hands the check to Holly, and YoYo ratchets it up: *wuuffffooouuu ... wuuffffooouuu* ... These barks are similar to the previous barks but more intense. His back legs are bent, and he's using rigid front legs to support those barks. Mr. Mitchell quickly draws back his hand. A sound comes from the audience. It's a faint *wuuffff ... wuuffff*. An imitation—coming from a redheaded boy in the bleachers. He does it perfectly, too, and takes it up at the end into a howl. YoYo looks in that direction and responds with an equally muted *wuuffff ... wuuffff*. The boy sends a *wuuffff ... wuuuffff* back.

YoYo answers again, and now the boy is joined by several other children, all *wuuffffffing* in unison. YoYo is so excited that he responds with a continuous multibark: *wuuffff ... wuuffff ... wuuffff ... wuuuffff*. All the children in the audience return barks that can be heard in the next county. YoYo takes up the challenge, puts his head up, and out comes a high-pitched squeal. *Oooouuuuueeeeeee*. Really! And it's soprano. It could have been a high C. I didn't know it was in his repertoire. A boy with braces and a perfect falsetto mimics that squeal. I record every word because I know the Committee will enjoy studying this rich communication. Communication? It's a conversation, and heaven only knows what words are hidden in there. Another child in the audience imitates his *Oooouuuueeeee*, and YoYo begins to dance around on his stand.

That's it. There they go. The children jump up, dancing and squealing. The audience laughs and claps at the spontaneity of it. Even BoBo, who watched silently, stands up and adds his woof. That's a yes, of course, since he wants to join the fun.

Holly enjoys it too, but she knows the program has to keep moving. She picks YoYo up to silence him and stretches her hand out for the check Mr. Mitchell holds in midair. Laughing, he hands it to her. The whole place comes alive with laughter. It's that kind of day. Holly chuckles and steps to the microphone.

"Mr. Mitchell, I am sure you heard YoYo and BoBo, too, thank you for the Bank of Freedom's generosity. I think I heard them say they want the check to go to the Holiday Humane Society, where all dogs are kept until they have found a home ... a good home."

Wait a minute. I think Holly takes great liberties here with that translation. In fact, I'll bet my wing bumpers that those barks were not thanking the president. I'll translate them to prove my point: YoYo's first bark—the top of the line *wooofffff*—was a clear warning to Mr. Mitchell when he put his hand out to pet him. But Mr. Mitchell didn't behave correctly. He didn't go into a submissive position. When he didn't comply, YoYo went into attack mode with body language and complained about the noncompliance.

Then, when he heard the children imitate him with their little *wufs*, he played with them because he knew they weren't threatening. How did he know? Because dogs can tell from sounds how big the body is that they came from. It's another evolved ability that identifies whether the body size is threatening. In other words, he knew the little *wufs* came from little people.

Next, the soprano squeal wasn't a dangerous scream. His lips weren't retracted. No teeth were bared. Instead, his head was back, singing notes up and down and then reaching for the C. My take: it was a yodel. *Yo-de-la-de-oo*, musical and joyous. And contagious, I might add, because we heard the chorus of yodels that followed. I wonder: can an aria be far behind?

Now it's the captain's turn. All gussied up in a fancy dress uniform, he strides with military posture to the podium and stands next to YoYo, who looks minuscule next to the six-foot-four-inch cop. With a gravelly voice that reeks of authority, he begins.

"Well, a lot has already been said, but I have one important thing to add to the recognition of what this little pooch did on May 5, 2011."

Do I hear contempt in "little pooch?" I guess he can't help himself. It slipped out.

"This morning Juan Carlos Espinosa was arraigned on charges of attempted bank robbery, endangerment of citizens, discharging an unlicensed firearm, car theft, kidnapping, and child endangerment."

The audience gasps at the number of charges. Well, I knew he was a bad dude.

"Bail was set at $100,000, and he was remanded to the jail hospital to recover from shooting himself twice. He was unable to secure bail, so he'll remain in jail until his trial."

As if they are conspirators, he leans over to YoYo, saying, "We don't have to worry about him causing any more trouble, do we, poochie? And we hope the district attorney will do his best to secure a conviction, don't we, so that your efforts will not have been in vain."

YoYo retreats to a far corner, putting as much distance between them as possible. I decline to record his thoughts.

"Our police force does its job every day in every way possible, and we welcome the efforts of good citizens including … ummmmm … Yorkshire terriers … in maintaining the rule of law. Many of our officers have met … ummm … YoYo … and given him the respect he deserves." The officers stationed by the platform nod in agreement, but I can see this is hard for the captain to say. However, he thinks he has to play the part.

The end justifies the means, and I did get in a dig about the ineffective district attorney I want to replace.

"Our dedicated officers know what it takes to put oneself in harm's way. What that little pooo … dog did, they do every day."

Caught yourself just in time, didn't you? Just say his name, for heaven's sake. Stop thinking the cops should be honored and not some ridiculous dog. And it's not a silly name. In other words, get over it.

He reaches for a handsome case, and drums begin a soft roll.

"On behalf of the Los Angeles Police Department, we hereby award YoYo this medal." He removes a badge on a gold chain, and reads the inscription: "Badge #1. YoYo. Honorary Police Dog."

There's a burst of applause, and the captain looks pleased with himself.

Things are looking up for me.

Oh? Take a look at who you have to give this award to, Captain. As if he heard me, he looks, and his pleased expression disappears. YoYo growls at him with fangs exposed. His nose jiggles like Jell-O, and his upper lip is curled. The *ggrrrrrrs* turn into *aaaffff … aaafffff … aaaffffff*s. It's the most disdainful sound I've ever heard. It's his warning bark. He is not going to let the captain come near him, so forget about hanging a medal on him. Holly understands the dilemma and whispers, "To put your medal on him, you have to pick him up—but carefully—because he won't bite if you're holding him."

Pick him up? Is the woman crazy? Does she think that's the image I want to project for my campaign—the candidate for district attorney holding a little pooch—with photographers ready to snap a picture that will be used against me? What will people think?

There is silence as everyone waits for the presentation. The band is confused, and the drums go silent.

Well, I guess I've faced worse situations in my twenty-two years as a cop. I have to figure out a way to do this so the little sucker doesn't bite me.

I think *sucker* is allowed.

He rests his left hand on the glass stand. Predictably, YoYo moves toward it. The captain slides his right arm around on the other side and scoops him up. Holly takes a relieved breath as the medal slips over

YoYo's head. It hangs directly over the mayor's medal, and the drums and trumpets explode. The captain is happy that he succeeded, but I have the urge to giggle because YoYo's face tells it all.

I'm just a small dog. You're huge. Okay. You win this round. But watch your ankles.

Ears are in the stand-up V's, and black eyes gaze at the captain. From a distance, they look like they're a perfect team, and that's the way everyone will remember it. But here's an amusing aside: the photograph of that moment makes the front page of the local newspaper. The captain looks, well, uncomfortable, to say the least. Someone pins it on the bulletin board at the station, and everyone smiles at the captain's gritted teeth and pained expression, as if he smelled something bad. It's not often the tough boss gives them something to laugh at.

Holly motions for him to hold YoYo up so everyone can see the medals. Both medals gleam in the sunlight and almost overwhelm YoYo's little head. With that, the audience goes crazy. Parents and teachers cannot hold the excited children back any longer. They rush to the platform, climb on it, and dozens of little hands reach out to pet YoYo. What's this I'm hearing? Gratitude? The captain surprises me.

I owe you, poochie. Big-time. It worked. You just helped me win the election.

He's so sure of himself. Little does he know what is in store for him. I flutter around him, cruising in and out of his aura. He shivers with the cold chill of a premonition.

I get the feeling that something else is in store for YoYo and me. I think it will be something dangerous.

Right, my Captain, *this* story isn't over yet. It's just begun.

Chapter Five

Monday, Noon

Uh-oh. Just realized I screwed up. They warned me, but I did it again. I bet my wing bumpers, of all things. I can't believe I did that. If the Committee catches me …? Betting my wing bumpers was stupid, because I do tend to speed. In fact, I arrived here from the Dimension in a millisecond. In my whole life, I never drove a car over sixty. Now it's fun to open up the throttles, figuratively speaking.

I want to delete my gaff. But when I was taught how to do this report, they showed me how to enter but didn't mention anything about delete. Is this a sting? Off the record—at best, it's sneaky. They must know my weakness for Vegas. Well, I'll try erasing it before they catch it. I'll close my eyes, concentrate, and say "delete" a couple million times, and at the same time rev up wing energy … I hope it worked. It would be a disaster if they recalled me before I had a chance to prove that YoYo has crossed the bark barrier. When I do learn how, the first thing deleted from my vocabulary will be the words "I bet." Might as well. It's bye-bye Las Vegas for me, anyway.

In the meantime, I've been advised that the assignment has taken a different angle—in addition to the study. It could mean involvement with terrorists. Yes, I said "terrorists." I do like diversification. My life was predictable and boring, and this could be interesting. But I don't understand the transition from my study of *Canis familiaris* and its potential for speech to terrorists who want to blow up people and things. Far be it for me to question the Committee, but isn't that a bit of a stretch? It's hard to believe that any dog would be effective in a situation with terrorists, let alone a tiny Yorkshire terrier who was given the name of YoYo because it rhymes with BoBo. I can't imagine how this is going to turn out, and I hope it doesn't interfere with proving that YoYo can speak. My reputation in the Dimension is at stake. But with the assumption that the Committee doesn't make mistakes, I proceed as ordered. Terrorists, take note.

Here they are, in a secluded section of a rooftop. They face east and speak in a foreign language. That further complicates things. It's okay, though, because the Committee sends a translation. They're saying the Morning Prayer, the first of five throughout the day. The two men rise and pick up their rugs, and we descend into a small apartment three floors below. I float along on one of the rugs.

Phew! Their apartment has a strong metallic odor. The few pathetic pieces of furniture include a kitchen table covered with a large architectural drawing of a federal building. I recognize it. We passed it when we went shopping for Holly's new blouse. The lean thirty-five-year-old, Ali Rachman, who declared jihad at thirteen, sits at the table and studies the drawing. Piercing dark eyes and a long nose dominate his shaved face, now without the thick black mustache and beard.

He has a chubby younger brother, Omar, who wants to help Ali. He walks to the window and closes the blinds. Yesterday they caught one of the neighbors peeking, and today someone in the hallway asked whether they smelled anything strange. The brothers didn't speak but simply shook their heads and continued into their apartment. To speak would reveal their heavy accents. They want to avoid attention. It could lead to their apprehension and the failure of their mission. Yes, these guys have a mission, all right. They want their leader, Sheik Mohammed ali Kalii, released from a supermax federal penitentiary in Colorado and flown to Nimbaba. Now I know what their goal is, yet what part YoYo could possibly have in this plot is still a mystery to me.

These guys want to get the sheik out of prison because they have no one who can take his place. Thank the Celestials for that. One of them on this earth is enough. They think no one has his cunning and brilliance, which is so crucial to the growing influence of their movement, AFSTRAM. Its ultimate goal is world domination. I've gotta say, these guys are ambitious, but they look like a couple of twerps to me. However, they do have a mininuclear bomb—a warhead—stashed right here in this apartment. Did I say "mininuclear bomb"? What on earth is that? I thought it took a giant missile or a bomber to carry a nuclear bomb. One certainly wouldn't fit in this apartment.

I'm advised that I'm wrong. Not up-to-date on the latest developments. I just found out about something called a "suitcase bomb." The info is on the homeland security news website. It gives the possible dimensions as 14" x 16" x 8" with a critical mass of U-233. Oh my. Even I know that that much plutonium in a small bomb would cause a huge explosion. To me, it looks like a simple device—a tube or canister with two pieces of uranium. It's amazing that all you have to do is ram them together and voilà! You get your blast. No mushroom cloud, but lots of radioactive material is released into the air. While tucked in the suitcase, it's powered by a battery that's connected to the canister, and the whole contraption is sealed in lead. That makes it a heavy suitcase. But a thick layer of lead prevents leakage of radiation. Homeland security checks radiation levels constantly throughout the country. Any leakage would be detected and the plot exposed. Before detonation can take place, the device for firing has to be decoded. That can be done remotely. One of those gadgets on the floor next to them could be a detonator.

Here's the bottom line. The force of a low-level ten to twenty ton explosion would kill lots of people, but the radiation would be even more dangerous. If it were released into a densely populated city, thousands would die from radiation sickness during the weeks and months after exposure. So the real purpose of this suitcase bomb is to damage—no, destroy—the capitalist economy. That means I've got to find that suitcase. Let's see … where should I look? It's not in the refrigerator … not in the toilet tank or the shower. Nope, it's under the bed. How imaginative! The last place anyone would look. And it's not just one suitcase. There are two of them. They plan to double the destruction. A holocaust.

Ali reviews the plan with Omar. "Let's go over this. I don't want any mistakes."

Omar looks downcast. He knows what Ali means. He's afraid Omar will screw up the mission.

"It's a two-stage plan, remember?"

Of course Omar remembers.

How could I forget? It's what we've been working on for a month. Didn't I help you get the plans so you could analyze the schedules and activities of a twenty-four-hour period?

"Yes, Ali, I remember. You marked the security systems with those red Xs." He points at the drawing on the table.

"Right. And concluded that, with a good plan, it is possible to take over the federal building. The first stage of the plan is an incendiary bomb. We use it as a diversionary tactic—start a fire—to get into the building with the suitcases."

Omar jumps in. "And then we take over the building. That means we're ready for the next step—stage two of your plan—to use the nukes strategically. Either they release the sheik, or we blow up the building, along with the hostages. All we have to do is show them the detonators strapped to our wrists."

Omar reaches down and picks up one of the contraptions. Ali takes it from him.

"I'm going to put the code in now. There can't be any mistakes."

He enters 911/II and picks up the second detonator.

"See how simple it is. But beautiful. That's why they give us all the support we need."

He means financial support from AFSTRAM—the money that keeps flowing to terrorists throughout the world.

"Do you realize, little brother, that if we succeed, we could destroy the evil capitalist economy? At least, we'll severely damage it," Ali says with satisfaction.

Omar isn't so sure. In fact, he rarely understands Ali's plans. His confusion and predictable clumsiness annoy Ali, but he puts up with Omar. He needs Omar for the mission. What an interesting relationship: using someone of whom you're contemptuous to kill people. For sure, it's not founded on brotherly love.

"It wasn't easy getting those materials into a federal building, since they put in all those incendiary detectors. But we outfoxed them, didn't we? By pretending to play soccer while we checked out the exterior of the building. It paid off, too, little brother, when we found that small opening."

Last week they did find an open vent and used a stick to push the packet into the building. It contains the materials for the incendiary bomb—aluminum-sulfur pellets, I believe, with an igniter, a fuse, and a delay mechanism that they'll set to blow up in the middle of the night and start a fire. I hope I got all that right, because this is new to me. Quite different from the knit one, purl two I'm used to.

This morning they go through security at the entrance of the building. No problem for them and certainly none for me as I follow, flitting over the guard, and glide beside them. They pass the elevators and detour to the hall, hoping to find the packet still in the vent. Omar is the lookout. Ali waits for some people to leave. Then he walks to the vent but sees that it has a screen. He twists and tugs to get the screen off, but it resists.

"Omar," he hisses. "Come here and open this."

Omar has big hands, and he quickly pulls the screen off and moves back into position. Ali extends his arm into the vent. He feels the packet at his fingertips, but it's just out of reach. Omar frantically signals that someone is coming. A desperate Ali sinks to his knees and pushes his arm in as far as possible. He pulls the packet out as a woman walks into the hall.

"Tripped," Ali says to her, smiling as he brushes off his pants. She smiles back and keeps walking.

They inspect the packet, find it intact, put the screen back, and take an elevator to the third floor, where they enter an empty restroom and assemble the incendiary device.

"Let me see what you've done," Ali says to Omar, who sighs. He knows Ali doesn't trust him and will check his work.

"Aha." Ali finds a loose connection and gives Omar a look that says, "Why can't you get it right?" Omar's feelings are hurt. It doesn't matter how hard he tries; he can never please his brother. Ali attaches the device to the back of a stall door where it will explode and start a fire in the middle of the night. That's Stage One of the plan. Omar takes a sheet of paper out of his pocket, unfolds it, and tapes it to the stall door. He reads aloud, "Out of Order," but thinks, *Hey, look at that! I got it right.*

They return to their apartment. I'm not surprised when Ali cautions Omar not to go near the nuke detonators, but he doesn't have to worry. Omar's not looking forward to using them. I take wing and return to home base to wait for Stage One of the plan to unfold.

Monday, 7:00 p.m.

It's time for YoYo's and BoBo's evening walk in the park. The dark-green, freshly cut grass is fragrant. Well-trimmed, handsome trees offer a little shade for those hot days of summer. The city doesn't just maintain the park—they manicure it. It's one of the prettiest parks I've ever seen, including those in different galaxies that specialize in parks. Holly lets them run off their leashes and play with all the dogs in the neighborhood. Here comes Willow, a six-month-old Airedale. She's headed for Pepsi, a year-old Lab mix. Now I get to watch how one dog invites another to play. It's a standard ritual.

Willow begins by running to Pepsi and goes face-to-face, nose-to-nose with her. She slaps the ground with her front paws. They hit with a "plop." Pepsi wags her tail in response. Willow bends her front legs to a kneeling position, and her rump goes up in the air. It looks like she's bowing to Pepsi. She wags her tail enthusiastically. This ritual has facial expressions too. Willow's eyebrows are raised, her mouth is open, and no teeth are bared. In dog language, it's, "Hello. Wanna play with me?"

"Sure," says Pepsi, wagging back, and they begin a mutual but restrained biting that is accompanied by the most ferocious sounds. They run, chase each other, and pause frequently to take stock. Heads nod as if they are asking, "You okay? I'm okay. Let's rumble." They tumble and try to outrace each other, take turns attacking, bark nonstop, and tackle like any football player. Every dog owner has undoubtedly seen this, but I'll bet only a few have realized how structured the dog play ritual is.

Sometimes Willow plays with YoYo. Already, she's about ten times bigger than he is, but I think Willow handicaps herself. Big dogs will do that when they play with smaller dogs or children. Willow rolls over on her back so YoYo can pretend dominance. He's not gracious about it, either. He sits on her tummy and gnaws at her throat until she gets tired or bored and takes off. There's no way he can catch her. I save those images and frequently replay them in slow motion to enjoy the nuances of their fair play. I don't need a DVD or Blu-ray to do it, either. It's one more advantage of being a resident of the Dimension. We're beyond electronic gadgets. Steve Jobs is definitely in heaven.

The park isn't far from the terrorists' apartment. I probably should expect something to happen pretty soon, but I dread YoYo's possible involvement. Just because he took down a bank robber doesn't mean the little guy can deal with terrorists. Meanwhile, he has fun playing ball. Holly tosses the ball for BoBo, and YoYo intercepts it. BoBo chases him until he gets it back.

Seeing them play together I notice a big improvement. Until recently, YoYo was so protective of Holly, he considered BoBo an intruder. If BoBo got near Holly, YoYo subjected him to a litany of yips and snarls accompanied by a series of leaps at his nose. BoBo either plowed over him like a tank or simply pushed him away with a gentle thrust of his head and moved in for his share of petting. I should mention that BoBo's head is about the same size as YoYo's body.

There's another sign of improvement: YoYo now tolerates Ted, Holly's husband, getting near her without biting his ankles, allowing previous bites to heal. Julie, YoYo's groomer, cries out, "YoYo, that hurt!" when she gets nipped, but Ted never does. He points to the blood on his ankles. "See that? See that? Your little rat dog did that."

Hearing someone call my sweet puppy a "rat dog" is really hard on me. But when I think about it, I have to admit that Ted's right because Yorkshire terriers were bred in the 1800s to control rats infesting the coal mineshafts and grain silos in England. Then they were used for hunting—to chase small game out of their burrows. Ultimately, they found their way into homes and onto laps like mine. Today, Yorkies are one of the most popular small breeds. To that, add expensive. And heart-stealers. He stole mine, and I can see now that he's got Holly's.

Holly is about to throw the ball again, but there's a big ruckus. It's YoYo furiously leaping and barking at the fence—at the two men dressed in black who are loading items into a sedan next to the fence. Those men are the terrorists and the subject of my new assignment. So contact is made, and the adventure, whatever it will be, begins. There's a lot at stake now, the least of which is my potential reward: the upgrade or the wish. For now, that's on the backburner.

The terrorist plan starts tonight when the incendiary bomb explodes in the federal building. Ali and Omar wait for the fire department to rush into the building, and, wearing the uniforms I saw hanging in their closet, they join the firemen with those detonators strapped to their wrists. The suitcases with the bombs are small enough to be concealed under the big yellow coats. They'll hide until the building returns to normal. Tomorrow morning they'll emerge, threaten to detonate the bombs, and take control of the building.

Ali will make the call to the attorney general, with the message: "Release the sheik and fly him to Nimbaba. Then we will release the hostages." Hah! Both Ali and Omar know that even when the sheik is free, they still have another mission to carry out—their final one.

At the moment, the fence shakes and rattles as YoYo hurls his little body against it. This park is now his territory, and he defends it with the most stringent of warnings: *Aawwwfffff ... Aaaawwwwfffff*.

It starts out high broadband, descends in the middle, and the volume goes way up at the end. Almost a scream. There's a lot of body language, too, as he amplifies the volume and running speed that send a signal to the other dogs: "Enemy invasion. Come help." Toys are dropped, and all the dogs run to join the charge. They growl, bark, and howl. YoYo understands that barking is contagious for dogs, and he uses it to manipulate the other dogs into joining him in the session.

Ali snarls something at them: *"Allahummahdini fiman hadayt, wa afini fiman afayt wa tawallani fiman tawallayt, wa barik li fima a tayt. Wa qini sjarra ma qadayt, fa innaka taqdi wa la yuqda alayk."*

He glares at them with hatred and kicks the fence. Now there's bedlam.

While I wait for a translation, Ali strides to his car, throws some hats—the hats that firemen wear—in the backseat, and drives away. The bombs are stashed in the trunk.

YoYo continues to attack the fence. It reminds Holly of the bank incident: *Thank goodness they left. I certainly don't want YoYo attacking a fireman.*

Of course she doesn't have a clue what part her dog will play in this drama. But then, neither do I.

Here's someone who understood what Ali said. He puts his dog on its leash and hurries out of the park. No wonder, after he hears, "If I ever see you again, little dog, I will strangle you. I will put my knife into your foul, dirty little body and twist. I will cut out your tongue. I will chop off your head. Praise Allah so that I will do this."

Yeah, yeah, yeah! Ali doesn't know who he's dealing with.

Monday, 11:45 p.m.

Holly is sleeping, and YoYo snuggles up to her. BoBo's curled up in his crib. That's what they call his down-lined basket. I know the detonation is taking place and hover nervously, flitting about the room, unable to settle into my usual spot in the speakers. YoYo jumps off the bed. His ears are up. They rotate like radar antennae. He hears sirens screaming in the distance. BoBo doesn't stir. At thirteen, his hearing isn't too good. The neighborhood dogs howl in response to the sounds that vibrate painfully in their ears. The cacophony continues and finally wakes Holly.

Something's happened. If it's a fire, it's a big one.

When the sirens finally stop, YoYo jumps back on the bed. BoBo continues to snore. But Holly can't sleep. She vividly remembers every detail of the episode in the bank. She still has nightmares of the Glock pointing at her and YoYo. I can't settle down, either. I prepare to go bicoastal by engaging the system that allows me to be in two places at once. Or three or four, if necessary. It's not difficult if you understand time and space. Humans have to go a lot further than "high tech" to catch up. The Committee was encouraged to hear that humans were toying with the theory that there are other universes that are connected by a string. That's an impressive sign of human progress and creativity. But now, after experiencing enlightenment on the tour of the Dimension, I realize that they have a long way to go and could use a couple more

Einsteins. Getting around on strings sounds primitive, limiting. I don't want to sound like a snob, but the truth is that I can go to any universe I choose with these trustworthy wings.

It was quite a surprise to learn about the other universes—unlimited universes—that range from massive to micromini, offering opportunities for unending exploration. I've done some in the short time I was there and hope to do more when—and if—I go back. I still hope for a chance to stay with YoYo. In the context of universes, it's amazing that the Committee considers that a dog saying words is important. Well, if the Committee thinks so, it must be very important, so I stay vigilant and ready to document what will surely be a duel between David and Goliath. Or YoYo and Ali. We'll discount Omar.

Chapter Six

I zip across the country and land on the desk of the attorney general. My timing is perfect. The hotline is ringing. His staff rushes into his office. That ring means trouble. He answers, switching on the speaker, and hears Ali's speech.

"Good afternoon, sir. We are members of AFSTRAM, and we have control of your federal building in Los Angeles. Hundreds of your citizens will remain our hostages until you release Sheik Mohammed ali Kalii from prison. Then you must fly him to Nimbaba."

The attorney general and his staff exchange looks. They know AFSTRAM is a militant jihadist group based in Nimbaba.

"Unless you release the sheik, we will detonate our nuclear bombs. If you attempt to capture us, we will detonate those bombs."

"Nuclear bombs? How is that possible?" General Vandersal responds, doubtful that it was possible to get any kind of explosive into a federal building with the heavy security that's in place.

"Yes, bombs that we brought in, piece by piece, substance by substance, mostly through your southern border. No problem! We pay coyotes, and they do what we tell them."

The attorney general closes his eyes, thinking that his worst nightmare has come true. The staff grimaces at the bad news.

"We built two minibombs. Your homeland security calls them

'suitcase bombs.' We have them with us. A detonating device is at our fingertips. I will be clear. Number one: if anyone tries to enter this building, we will detonate these bombs. Number two: if the sheik is not free in Nimbaba by 0230, we will detonate those bombs. That gives you eighteen hours. Here's the good news, Mr. General: at 0231, if the sheik is free, we will release the hostages. These are your choices."

The click tells the attorney general the conversation is over, and Vandersal reaches for the line that connects him directly with the president as he barks orders to his staff.

"We prepared for this. We have a plan. Put it into action." Key staff members rush to start the process. Speaking to aides in his office, the attorney general considers the prospect of meeting the deadline.

"The sheik is in the supermax in Florence, Colorado. We have an air force base right next to it at Colorado Springs. That will save some time. It will take sixteen hours in the air to get to Nimbaba, which leaves us less than two hours to get the sheik on a plane."

"Can we do it?" an aide asks.

"Yes, we can." He answers with more confidence than he feels.

That's a good attitude, Mr. Attorney General: can do. Only I wish I could tell you that you may get some special help—from a small terrier. At least I think you may, knowing what I know about YoYo. But even if I could tell you, you'd never believe me. All I know is, I wouldn't be here, fluttering over your desk, if YoYo wasn't going to be a player.

With the general's command, a vast network of activity is set in motion through many departments of the government—especially Homeland Security.

Minutes later, an FBI unit hurries to secure the release of the sheik from the penitentiary. The Pentagon alerts the air force at the nearby Colorado Springs airport. The sixteen-hour flight limits the number of planes suitable for the task. The decision is made to use the B-2 Stealth bomber, which may require midair refueling because of the speed necessary to meet the deadline.

The attorney general doesn't like it. "It adds to the risk factor," he tells his aides, but there is no better alternative. The most experienced pilot on the base is chosen for the flight, and he races to the airport to check out the B-2. For some reason, I like its name: Spirit.

An hour and a half later, the sheik arrives with the agents assigned to accompany him, and Spirit is ready for takeoff. A team of special-ops marines are on board.

In Los Angeles, control center units move near the federal building. The entire area is secured. By 11:30 a.m., local time, John Travis, a senior FBI agent with experience in hostage situations, takes command of the unit, which includes SWAT teams, FBI agents, and police from local units.

Thank heaven the Committee provided me with this bicoastal system, plus additional wingspan that allows me to flip all over the country. It's critical now because of the need to monitor Ali and Omar, keep track of John Travis's efforts, and, most important, pay close attention to any sounds that YoYo makes. If YoYo starts chatting, I'll glom on to every word. The Committee's continuing confidence in me could mean I'm off the hook and won't be recalled. I hope I'm up to such a huge challenge, but I must say that YoYo seems willing to accept all challenges, as long as Holly doesn't run of cookies. As for me, this is better than sitting at home knitting scarves that no one ever wore. I'm eager to proceed.

John Travis also has a tough assignment: prevent the detonation of the bombs and free the hostages without endangering the community. To forestall any panic, the public has not been informed that the terrorists have mininukes in the federal building. There is still some time to work out the problem.

At 1:45 p.m., local time, the radiation and biological weapon detecting units are in place. John dials the reception desk in the federal building. Ali answers.

"It's about time you called. We know you've taken Sheik Mohammed ali Kalii from his cell. There is nothing for us to talk about until he is on a plane headed for Nimbaba." He hangs up.

John pushes the redial button and lets the phone ring until Ali picks up.

"If you want your sheik, you *will* talk to me. Once the plane takes off, you must surrender. The bombs must be disarmed. On this we will not negotiate."

Ali laughs. "Oh, is that all you want? Well, here's the bad news. No negotiation, no surrender, no disarming, until the sheik is safe in Nimbaba—in the hands of our people. Then we'll be happy to open doors and release hostages. By the way, the hostages saw the suitcases with the bombs. I don't think they'll try to escape or help you."

That's true. At 8:15 a.m., Ali and Omar emerged from hiding, dumped the yellow coats, and stashed the suitcases. The guards in the building were taken by surprise. Threats were expected to come from outside, and once they saw the detonators on Ali and Omar's wrists, they had no choice but to surrender. Along with the terrified hostages, they were herded to the sixth floor, where they sit in groups. The hostages did note the detonators on the terrorists' wrists and saw the suitcases. But they don't know how potentially deadly the contents are, and the guards don't want to alarm them even more. Of course, they immediately called 911 on their cell phones and were referred to specially trained agents who were ready to assure them that a coordinated effort to rescue them was in motion. Few are reassured. Some talk to their families, while others cry or pray in the dark, since electricity to the building has been turned off.

News travels fast. Bad news is supersonic. TV and radio stations begin reporting that terrorists are holding hostages in the federal building on the west side. No reporters are allowed in the secured area, but the pressure is on. Facebook shuts down, and an overloaded Internet collapses.

Ali continues his ultimatum. "We will surrender when our sheik is free, but we will plead for mercy and demand to be tried—not by your corrupt government, but by a world court that understands how our people are victims of your capitalism and degenerate society. On that you have my promise."

"Promise?"

"I promise on my mother's honor."

Why do I not believe Ali? Because he smiles and winks at Omar, who swallows hard and looks away. Omar knows what is really going to happen to him. For him, it's nothing to smile about. He differs from Ali. He's not ready to die yet.

John understands what the real message is. He hangs up and turns to the group surrounding him.

"They're going to detonate the bombs even if we release the sheik! We have to find a way into that building."

Chapter Seven

Tuesday, 2:30 p.m.
The Federal Building

The SWAT team begins the slow crawl, two men to the east side of the building, two men to the west. They lie prone on the ground and use their elbows to propel themselves forward while staying out of view of the building's big windows. At 3:01 p.m., they begin to check the entrances to the basement, the loading docks, the service elevators, and the air vents, but everything is shut tight. The security system is sensitive and would announce any intrusion. That eliminates the doors or the roof as possibilities. Just tapping the outside walls can trigger the alarms, which go off even with minor earthquakes. Next, the teams move to check the north and south sides, looking for an opening, a crevice—anything that will allow them an undetected presence in the building.

4:10 p.m.

The team reports: no openings. No cracks. Except that Sgt. Cameron and his partner found an exposed vent that may not be secured. The other team members crawl to examine it. Lt. Anderson uses his torchlight and sees that the vent goes about seven feet into the building. There's no sign of it being secure, but it has a screen on the inside. He advises Control of the find, and a few minutes later, they hear from headquarters: "That vent leads to a hallway in the west side of the first floor. No indication that it's secured. Proceed with screen removal. Keep vibrations to a minimum. Advise when operation is complete."

Using stealth and a variety of special tools, they cut the screen, and the alarms don't go off. So far, so good. They wait for further orders. Lt. Anderson, a tall, rugged ex-Marine, handpicked his team for this job. He wanted the strongest, most courageous men. Sgt. Jackson is as fit as an athlete with amazing reflexes that he has used many times in tight situations. Sgt. Gonzales, a decorated veteran, saw lots of action in Iraq, is steady, and handles stress well. Sgt. Cameron, the youngest member of the team, is enthusiastic, eager, and loves his job. Oh, I see. He also loves his cat, Meow. He talks about her incessantly. He's single, so Meow is probably his family. I understand perfectly. And I am perfectly happy to be with all these hunks. No, I'm not ashamed of admitting that. I may be dead, but there's no rule against thinking like a girl.

The group at the control center is encouraged with the find. They consider the options.

"That vent can be used for entry into the building."

"What entry of what?" is the question.

"Whatever we use to get in that building, it has to be very small. Even smaller than the robots available. The Pentagon is working on a pocket-size drone. It's in the shape of a hummingbird with six-and-a-half-inch wings that flap. It can fly eleven miles an hour, hover, fly sideways, backward and forward, and is equipped with a camera. It would be perfect for this mission, except it's not operational yet. It's just a prototype, and that doesn't leave us with many options."

"What about K-9?" someone asks.

"Yeah. That's a good idea. They're using fox terriers now for drug sniffing."

"I have a fox terrier. A small one. He weighs twenty-two pounds. I don't think he'd fit in a six-inch vent."

"Well, we've got to come up with something—something new, something different—that's never been done before."

"Got to think outside the box."

"Yeah, way outside," Agent Ruth Winehouse adds.

John is staring hard at someone. Someone who got his attention because he has a silly grin on his face. At a time like this, it's unbelievable. Except that it's that dreadful Captain MacDonald. Him again! John knows the captain is running for district attorney and has made quite a reputation for himself. But he's at a loss to understand how anyone could be smiling now. John is about to find out because, as usual, the captain sees an opportunity. Here he goes.

"Well, John, I believe that tonight, after SWAT teams parachute onto the roof and grounds all around the building, the decision will be whether to force entry into the building and risk detonation, or to find a way to use that small vent opening." He pauses and looks around at the people in the room, seeing confirmation of his assessment, before announcing, "I just may have a solution."

It's obvious the captain is thinking about the robbery at the bank foiled by YoYo. Now I've got the connection I needed to understand the direction this is taking. The captain still fumes at how the mayor upstaged, outmaneuvered, and sabotaged his plan. This situation could be another opportunity to help his campaign. So he's going to suggest that they use YoYo.

Poochie can be counted on to make trouble and distract the terrorists. Only this time, if we can get him in the building, I will be in control. Even a few minutes of YoYo time will give the team the opportunity they need. If they get in, they have a chance. And this time, if my idea works, I'll make sure my name is on the lips of every newscaster in the country. Sure, I want to save the hostages, the city, the economy, but God knows I desperately want to be district attorney.

Okay, thanks to the captain and his confessed ambition, now we know that YoYo will be involved. What I can't figure out is how they'll manage to get him into that small opening. We'll wait and see what human ingenuity can do. If they succeed, it will be YoYo versus the terrorists. And he's just a little dog. That's hard for me. But I must remain the spectator and recorder of events that might reveal evolutionary progress. Especially if YoYo asks, "Why me?"

The captain has everyone's attention now.

"Here's my idea for a solution. Now don't laugh. I have a story to tell. After you hear it, you can decide whether it's a crazy idea or whether maybe, just maybe, a little Yorkshire terrier named YoYo can work a miracle."

Chapter Eight

One minute everyone in the control room is dead serious, and the next, they're laughing their heads off at the story of YoYo's escapades in the bank. Even the SWAT team listening on the radio chuckle at the terrier's antics.

The captain's presentation is an edited version of the mayor's performance, and he's proud of the imitation. He thinks he's learned the tricks of politics and has graduated from being a dumb flatfoot.

"So what do you think of *my* idea?" He has no intention of letting this opportunity pass by him.

John shakes his head in amazement. "Unless someone has a better idea, I say let's go for it. Worst-case scenario, we get him in the building, and the terrorists see a little dog. How bad can that be? At least we're doing something while we keep working on other solutions."

No one disagrees.

"Okay. We'll try it. But we need a strategy. While we work on that, someone has to find this dog—YoYo?—and bring him here."

Officer Bonner comes forward. "It better be me. I know them, but believe me, it isn't going to be easy. The woman's attached to that dog. I don't know whether she can be convinced to sacrifice him." He finds her number on a computer and dials.

Holly's cell phone rings as she oversees Julie grooming YoYo. He gets a nice, warm bath with flea shampoo on his body and non-irritating baby shampoo for his head. Blunt-pointed scissors cut his topknot and muzzle into a short, squared shape. The long fur on V-shaped ears gets trimmed. Now they look like butterfly wings. YoYo didn't mind that, but he isn't too happy when she shaves off his floor-length coat with an electric razor. Well, the long fur picked up leaves and twigs in the garden, carried them into the house, and deposited them on the carpet. Now his coat is short—and so soft, it feels like velvet.

Ted sees the sheared look another way and tells Holly, "Now you really have a rat dog."

Ted and YoYo still have a somewhat adversarial relationship. They did have a rocky start. Ted won't admit to it, but I believe he is jealous of all the affection Holly gives YoYo. I've heard some of the unflattering names he calls YoYo, including "Rat Turd." When YoYo charges him, he says, "Go back in your hole, rat." It annoys me, but Holly rationalizes that it's his way of expressing affection. Hah!

After the grooming ordeal, Holly comforts YoYo with sweet talk and hugs. He reciprocates by licking her hand and working his way up her arm. She says, "That's enough, YoYo. I took a shower this morning." The phone rings, and she answers.

"Mrs. Hancock, this is Officer Bonner. We met during the bank robbery. I have a request from Captain MacDonald. He would like to meet with you as soon as possible."

Holly is immediately suspicious. *What's the captain up to now?*

She knows the big ceremony to give YoYo a medal had little to do with YoYo and was really about his wanting to win the election. She got that right! She had put the two medals on display in the living room, but every time YoYo passed them, he barked. The problem was resolved when she moved them into the guest bedroom.

"I have a doctor's appointment tomorrow, and I can stop in on the way."

"The captain said to tell you it's urgent. Very urgent."

"Okay, if it's that important, I'll leave right away."

"Drive to the station. I'll meet you there. Oh, and be sure to bring YoYo."

Yeah. As if she would go anywhere without YoYo. And BoBo too.

She washes her face, combs her hair, rubs on a little lip gloss, and puts on jeans and a T-shirt—her standard daily work uniform. YoYo watches her. He knows this ritual means she will leave. We know that dogs can hope, and he surely has expectations of being included in any outing. Dogs share a lot of other emotions with humans. They get depressed, sad, bored, jealous, curious, impatient, anxious, fearful, competitive, and greedy. There are also intellectual similarities. Both BoBo and YoYo have preferences. "I prefer steak to kibble." They make judgments and decisions. "I must investigate that noise—it could be a burglar." They decline. "No, I don't want to go to the vet." And they ponder: "When is she coming home?"

They have wish lists too. Here are a few from YoYo's list:

Wish #1. Mom, you know that chicken dish you make with all the herbs? You call it Chicken Tandori. I love the tidbits you save for me. Licking the plate is good too. While halfheartedly nibbling on bland kibble yesterday, I wished I could ask you to add some oregano and thyme to my dog food. To pick up the flavor a bit. Some pepper too. I love pepper. It's an antioccident—that would be good for me. You know how I lick all the plates clean, savoring every tiny morsel, especially when you cook with herbs. But no basil, please. I hate basil. Onions too. Would like more curries. But hold the chutney and coconut.

Wish #2. I don't understand why Christmas comes only once a year. I wish we could have more Christmases throughout the year. It's so much fun playing with the tree ornaments, pulling the light strings, and exploring the packages under the tree. Some of them are for me too. I sniff all the packages, searching for them. But don't make it too easy to find them. I like a challenge.

Wish #3. Hey, Mom. I wish that you would do me a favor. It's not a big thing, but I'd appreciate it. When you have to go to the vet, I wish you'd leave me at home. Give him my best regards, but I have no desire to visit his smelly chamber of torture and terror. Believe me, I'm looking forward to the day I don't have to squeal and whine when he sticks a needle in me. The day I can yell, "Ouch," I will love the look on that dude's face.

Wish #4.* You have no idea how frustrated I am in trying to communicate with you. There are so many things I want to tell you. I'd have some sharp retorts for your husband, too, if I could say the words. You ask me questions all the time, and I can't answer. That's so frustrating. It drives me crazy. Anyway, one of your friends gave me an idea. The one who frequently has bandages on her face. The last time she visited, she told us she had had her nose fixed. If she had her nose fixed, among numerous other fixes, why can't I have some too? A good plastic surgeon could probably loosen my tongue so I could wiggle it. Then I could manage those *t*'s and *d*'s. A lot of movie stars have work done on their lips. Surely they could refer me to a surgeon for a reconstruction. A few cuts and some filler would make my lips flexible. Then I'd be able to say *b*'s and *p*'s. Do you realize how many words would be possible? The conversations we could have? Am I just a scalpel away from this muteness?

Please note asterisk on #4 for priority.

How's that for creative thinking by a dog? Well, of course dogs think. It's about time humans realized that the process is not exclusive to them. "I think, therefore I am," also applies to *Canis familiaris*. And cats. Just ask any owner who's been punished for not fulfilling cat requirements.

Right now YoYo hopes that he'll be included in the outing Holly's getting ready for. He gets his wish when she puts his harness on him, and his tail wiggles happily. BoBo rouses from a deep sleep, and he's ready to go too. BoBo doesn't need a leash because he's a therapy dog and very obedient. He specializes in visits to senior citizens in hospitals. They love the way he leans against them for easy petting. The folks who are confined in beds or wheelchairs enjoy throwing the tennis ball, and BoBo tirelessly retrieves it for them. I wish he had visited me when I had my broken hip. On second thought, it might have made me sad and made me miss my Brandy even more.

Holly maneuvers the drive through dense lines of police cars. We are stopped, and she is asked for her ID. Then officers escort her to the station. Officer Bonner greets us when we drive into the parking lot.

"What's going on?" Holly asks. "It seems like every squad car in town is here."

Officer Bonner doesn't respond to her question. Instead he tells her, "The captain is in the control center. We have a situation going on. I'll take you there." He leads us to a squad car, puts Holly and YoYo in the front seat, and BoBo is relegated to the back. The door slams before I can flip in next to BoBo, so I ride the hood ornament. It's breezy but exciting. Cars scuttle out of our way when they see the flashing lights and hear the sirens.

"Oh my gosh. Does this have anything to do with the hostages in the federal building?" Holly asks.

He hedges again, answering as they pull up to the large mobile unit. "The captain will explain."

They're waiting for us. All eyes immediately go to the creature in Holly's arms. John shakes her hand and introduces himself. Holly settles into a chair; YoYo nestles in her lap. BoBo, an extrovert, makes the rounds and greets everyone with a wagging tail.

John explains the situation. "They'll detonate unless we meet their demands."

"Demands?"

"The sheik is the granddaddy of all terrorists. If released, he'll plot ways to kill innocent people, cripple the economy—he is relentless in his attacks against us. We didn't want to release him, but we had to. The terrorists gave us very little time. The plane has already taken off and will land in Nimbaba."

Holly interjects, "Then the hostages will be released."

"No, I'm afraid not. That's not how terrorists operate. After they get confirmation from their colleagues that the sheik is safe, they will detonate the bombs. They will commit suicide. The blast will kill those innocent people locked in the federal building. Even worse, radioactive material will rain on the city."

She probes. "How do you know they'll detonate the bombs?"

"How do we know? Because the terrorist swore on his mother's honor that he would surrender. That's what they always say when they're lying."

Holly is perplexed. *What does any of this have to do with me?*

It has little to do with you, my dear, and everything to do with our little YoYo.

"We heard the most amazing story about YoYo. How he foiled a bank robbery."

Here it comes, courtesy of the ambition-driven captain.

"We need a diversion to get our people in there to subdue the terrorists before they activate the bombs. We discovered a tiny opening in the building. We researched every possibility. It's the only option available right now. We believe we can maneuver YoYo through that hole and get him onto the first floor where the terrorists are. We'll use nightscopes and listening devices to track his activity. It's the only way to do this without alerting them. Even if they do see a small dog, they won't be alarmed. We have to take the chance that YoYo will do something to distract them—something that will allow us to rush in and subdue them before they can detonate the nukes. From what I understand, all he has to do is to be himself—a tough little warrior."

He reaches across Holly to pet him, and YoYo's lip curls up, baring his teeth. A *ooowwooff ... oowwooff* is a new sound. It sounds defiant and could mean that he understands what John is proposing. And objects. But there's no time to analyze those vowels and consonants. I'll replay it later.

John responds with admiration. "That's exactly what I mean."

Holly sits there, staring. She can't even speak.

Is he crazy? This is the most insane scheme I ever heard. This is the United States of America. We have the strongest military in the world. What about the army, the navy, the air force?

She glares at the captain.

These guys should be ashamed of themselves. Look at them ... the police, the FBI, the SWAT team—they have all the weapons, tools, technology in the world at their fingertips and they want to use my little dog? It's unbelievable. Not my little dog. Not YoYo.

She clutches him to her, looks into his sweet face, and plants a kiss on his head. It is true that they only see a dog who took down a robber. They have no concept of how lovable he is, how much joy he brings to her life, what he means to her. She strokes his head and rubs his back, now stubby with soft fur, and gets her voice back.

"You want me to sacrifice YoYo?"

"No, we don't. We want to get 360 people out safely, and when we do, YoYo will be with them. He won't be alone. Armed teams are ready to rush in and subdue the terrorists. We'll monitor the whole time. If it looks like the plan isn't working, we can bring him out. We get him in, we can get him out. Right now, YoYo is our only hope."

I must contradict you, John. I know you can get him in, but you don't have a clue how you could get him out.

A stunned Holly shakes her head no.

"I would like you to meet someone."

John nods at Agent Winehouse. She opens a door into a small room where a five-year-old boy sits. His rubs his tear-streaked face with fists. Ruth reaches for his hand and brings him into the room.

"This is Tommy Harper."

Tommy asks, "Can my daddy come home now?"

My heart—if I still had one, that is—goes out to him. His dad left him in the car early this morning when he went into the post office to mail a package. Now Dad is one of the hostages locked on the sixth floor.

"Not yet, honey. But there is someone here who might help your daddy come home. Want to meet him?"

The boy nods eagerly. Ruth points at YoYo sitting on Holly's lap. No wonder we love children. They are so intuitive, so trusting. That little fella rushes right over to YoYo, kneels in front of him, and looks into his black eyes.

"Can you? Can you save my daddy?" Salty tears drip onto YoYo. He tastes one and likes it. Dogs enjoy the flavor of salt. It's another thing they share with humans. They also like sweet things and appreciate bitter and sour flavors. No wonder herbs are on YoYo's wish list. YoYo continues to lick all the tears that flow, and Tommy interprets it as an answer. He leans into YoYo and whispers: "Thank you. Thank you." To the room he announces, "He's going to get my daddy back for me."

Holly's face pales. She closes her eyes to block out this heartrending scene. Her imagination takes over as she considers the possibility of letting them put YoYo into that building. Images flood in of YoYo in a dark hallway. She sees him stumble, hears him whine and cry. She doesn't want to think what the terrorists will do if they discover him. I get a signal from the Committee that it's time to intervene. I comply and slip into her mind some images of that day in the bank. She sees YoYo attack a nasty criminal, the battle that followed, and how YoYo won the battle. And all he had to do was be himself.

Somehow YoYo is unique. I feel it. There is something special about him. Maybe I should reconsider. If he does have a chance, even a small one, wouldn't I be selfish to prevent him from saving all those people?

If only I could tell her that YoYo was selected with much care and deliberation. It wasn't a lottery.

"Mr. Travis, I will agree to this on one condition. That I accompany YoYo to the building and stay the entire time he is in there. I will not leave him."

How I wish it had been possible for me to say those words to him.

The people in the room are dismayed at the idea. They believe she'll screw things up. But Holly did the right thing. YoYo definitely should not be abandoned. John thinks so too.

"Agreed. Okay. Now, Mrs. Hancock, how about taking a ride?" He orders his staff, "Let's get her suited up for the blimp. Fast."

Holly takes out her cell phone to call Ted. He doesn't answer, so she leaves a message. "Hi, darling. Going to be home a little late tonight."

Chapter Nine

Tuesday, 11:00 p.m.

We're floating over the city in a huge blimp—another exciting new experience for me. Now it hovers silently. We must be over the federal building. There's no moon tonight, so it's dark down there—where we're headed. Black-clad figures drop a rope ladder, scramble down, and run to the side of the building. Lt. Anderson takes a trembling Holly's hand, gently helps her onto the ladder, and she cautiously descends. She wears a backpack. In it is our precious YoYo, who will be sent on what I fear is a far more impossible mission than uttering some words. I don't see why they can't find an alternative solution. I ride a breeze down with her. We are met, and Holly is helped off the ladder. The lieutenant leads her to the opening where they plan to put YoYo.

"We cut the screen so it's open at the end." He inserts the torch so Holly can see where YoYo has to go. It's barely six inches wide. She's appalled.

How can they expect him to move in it for seven feet to get into the hall?

"This isn't going to work, Lieutenant. I'm sorry, but there is no way anyone can persuade him to go in there."

"Maybe not anyone, but how about any*thing?*"

He reaches for a small pouch that Sgt. Cameron hands him. My, my. The pouch squeaks when the sergeant opens it, and a tiny mouse pokes its head up. Its nose quivers, whiskers oscillate, and legs feverishly scramble to climb out. YoYo's sniff process goes into high gear. The scent tells him it's a mouse. To a terrier, that's prey. Nostrils flare, and he wiggles to escape from Holly.

"We owe the pleasure of this guy's company to Meow, who caught him. Sgt. Cameron rescued him before he became dinner."

This is a hoot. It's darn clever to use a mouse to entice YoYo. But I wonder, after the sergeant saved it from Meow, how did he know to tuck it in his pocket? And take it to work? Serendipity strikes again, or … we're being manipulated. Maybe my wish should be to get answers to all these questions.

"Yeah, I got there just in time. A few seconds later, there would have been no mouse. Boy, was Meow mad. I've got scratches to prove it," the sergeant adds. Holly smiles in spite of herself.

"That certainly is imaginative," Holly admits, lifting YoYo out of the backpack. She holds him tight for a moment. The team watches anxiously as she rubs his velvety coat and plants kisses on his head. She squeezes him tight and whispers, "Come back, YoYo. Remember you're a yo-yo. Come home to Mama."

The men are embarrassed by the display of emotion and turn away. When she sets him in the opening, he looks at the dark surroundings, confused, and mumbles some wwwaawwaaa's. Translated: *Why am I in here?* Or a reasonable facsimile.

I have mixed emotions about this. I wish YoYo could put his foot down and tell the lieutenant, "You first, fella."

When Holly nods, the lieutenant takes the mouse out of the pouch, wiggles it in front of YoYo and releases it. With jetlike speed, the mouse disappears into the tube. With a battle cry—*yaiyaiayiaiyai*—YoYo is barely a second behind. Sgt. Cameron inserts his nightscope and reports, "Demon dog has landed! Running east—full speed."

Demon Dog is the name they gave the mission, suggested by Captain MacDonald. He waits in the control center to hear whether his plot to use YoYo again has worked. That is, worked for his personal gain.

Sgt. Jackson listens with high-tech earphones and reports: "Silence. [Pause.] Now I hear something. Sounds like a scuffle. Hmmm. Hmmm. [Pause.] Silence. It's dead quiet now."

His emphasis is on "dead." So the strategy worked. The mouse got YoYo into the building. The team feels sorry for the mouse, but grateful. It made the ultimate sacrifice. However, I have my suspicions. It's not that I doubt YoYo's abilities. After all, he was bred to kill rats. I must see for myself, so I can report accurately. What am I saying! See? I'm here to listen. If ever YoYo will say something, it's when he has won a battle.

I slip through the convenient vent into the building, and hurry down the hall. I find YoYo and the mouse in an unbelievable scene. This is no ordinary mouse. Cornered, he stands on his hind legs and glowers at a surprised YoYo, who sits on his haunches to study this oddball mouse. He didn't expect a confrontation. The mouse suddenly squeaks, turns, and kicks its rear legs back like a bucking bronco. Then it jumps to the left. YoYo, not to be outdone, squeals, does a quick, fancy spin in the air, and also jumps to the left. They are still face-to-face, reminding me of two pugilists in a ring. The mouse crouches, its nose twitches, little beady eyes move furtively from side to side. Feet tap in place. Squeaking again, it jumps to the right. YoYo's nose twitches with excitement. Loud *HehHehHeh*s, and he leaps, spins, twirls a couple of times, and jumps to the right. He lands face-to-face with the mouse again. More *HehHehHeh*s. This routine continues several more times with a steady chorus of squeaks as counterpoint to the *HehHeh*s until the mouse decides to make a run for it. YoYo easily catches him, as he was bred to do, and holds him in his mouth. He shakes the mouse vigorously and tosses him into the air. The same thing he does with his toys. The mouse splatters onto the floor. YoYo and I wait to see whether the mouse moves. To him, it was a game, even though it didn't score as many *HehHehHehHeh*s as Stomp. He wants it to revive: *Come on, mousy, rise and shine. Don't play dead, and definitely don't go dead on me.*

After a long wait, we know the game is over. For the first time, he notices his surroundings and decides to investigate this long, dark hall. However, there is business to attend to. He sidles over to the wall and lifts his leg. A slender stream squirts out—just enough to mark the territory with his signature. It's valuable scent, and he's not going to squander it on one location. Dogs have unique bladders that allow them to save the balance for future markings, which are such an important part of dog communication. Minuscule dog messages can be left on trees, bushes, and fire hydrants. Sometimes even furniture becomes a bulletin board. Think of it as liquid e-mail. Human bladders work quite the opposite. Once the valve is open, there's not much choice.

That accomplished, YoYo wanders farther. Something catches his eye. It's a top from a soda bottle—interesting enough to sniff, lick, and savor the flavor. It's time for another marking. Up goes the leg. The exploration continues until he hears a familiar sound. His left ear, closest to the sound, does the rotation routine to identify it.

That sounds like Holly's toy. The one she always carries with her and talks to.

He heads in the direction of the lobby ... where the terrorists have set up shop. Ali and Omar sit at the reception desk. They have a good view of the windows and doors. Ali, stiff with tension, speaks on a cell phone.

"That's good news, Abdul. Call me when the plane lands." He turns to Omar. "They put Sheik Mohammed ali Kalii on the plane, and it took off. He's on his way. We won, little brother. We won the battle."

His face is so smug that I wish I could get permission to slap him. That is, if I had something to slap him with. I could zap his aura, but I will restrain myself—for now, anyway.

Ali, unaware of how close he came to having an unexpected spasm, joyfully announces, "Soon we will enjoy all those rewards in heaven."

Omar isn't so sure. He doesn't want to disappoint his big brother and tries to be happy about the prospects of dying, but visions of being blown to bits make him sort of ... well ... uncomfortable. Ali talks about the beautiful women they will have in the next life. Ali has a good imagination. Omar doesn't. He can't believe there are any women more beautiful or desirable than those he has seen shopping in Beverly Hills. He would trade the prospect of heaven for any one of them, except he thinks he doesn't stand a chance. Yes, we can spare a little sympathy for a terrorist whose family treats him as if he is stupid. True, he forgets a lot, stumbles, and says the wrong things. At five feet, four inches tall and two hundred pounds, he's no Brad Pitt, and he sure does like to eat. He knows he's overweight, but it hurts his feelings when they call him Obese Omar to his face.

He casts loving looks at their bag of supplies behind the desk. The bag contains the lunch their mother made for them before they left on this mission. It includes *kookoo morgh*, shish kebab, and *khoresh-e-gorme sabzi*. She wrapped them in plastic and slipped them into their bag alongside the explosives. Omar is thinking about the *khoresh*—his favorite—mentally savoring the flavor of a stew of lamb, beef, red kidney beans, onions, spinach, parsley, and herbs. Interesting herbs. I thought I knew all the herbs. I cooked with them all the time, but this *advieh* is new to me. It must be Middle Eastern.

The woman labored for hours cooking *kookoo morgh* for her sons, a saffron-flavored chicken dish made with eggs, onions, and lime juice. She even included a dessert—*rangeenak*, made with dates, walnuts, sesame seeds, cinnamon, and powdered sugar. They have a good mother, who doesn't want her boys to greet Allah on an empty stomach. They provided for her by carefully managing the generous funds from AFSTRAM that a messenger recently replenished, and leaving a substantial amount to sustain her after their mission is completed.

Sniff! Sniff! Sniff!

YoYo's picking up new fascinating scents drifting into the hall. His nose leads him into the lobby and directly to the bag with the food. As expected, he jumps on it and claws and scratches until the bag is open. On the trail of those enticing smells, he crawls inside the bag. But then he encounters the plastic wrapping, which stops him, but only for a moment. Again, he scratches, claws, and chews through it until he is into the food. Or about to be into it, because he hears someone approaching. It's Omar, headed for the bag. If he catches YoYo now, it would be a disaster. The whole mission, mine included, could end quickly. I want to warn YoYo to run for his life, but I can't move. My wings freeze when Omar picks up the bag. He is about to look into it, but we are saved—and not by a miracle. Ali does a "gotcha." He looks around and sees Omar with the bag. He knows what Omar's intentions are and snarls, "This is no time to think about food. Get to the window—I think I see a light out there. They may try something."

An embarrassed Omar drops the bag with a thud. Sheepishly, he takes the night-vision glasses from the desk and heads for the windows.

In the dark, he trips over a chair, falls into it, falls out of it, somersaults, and lands flat on his face.

Ali is extremely annoyed. He wonders how such a bumbler could be a member of his family. *It's a disgrace. There has to be a disconnect somewhere.*

Unable to contain his anger, he scolds, "Omar, for once in your life, *try* to do something right."

A humiliated Omar crawls to the windows, grimacing in pain. His back hurts, his ankle feels like it's broken. He wants to cry but instead reports, "I see—nothing."

Ali snarls back, "How can you see nothing?" further humiliating Omar, who has no answer. Ali turns away in disgust and dials his cell phone.

YoYo sits quietly inside the bag. He waits for someone to scold him. That's what usually happens when he explores. No one comes, so he proceeds to delve into the food, enjoying those wonderful flavors, especially the ones with his favorite herbs. For sure, he thinks, *Dog food was never like this.*

The shish kebabs are first. He likes the lamb and veggies but avoids the onions. Next, he devours the *khoresh-e-gorme sabzi* but spits out the kidney beans. Picky, picky! He looks at the *kookoo morgh*—the chicken smells so good—but he stops, unable to take another bite. All that food has made him sleepy, so he curls up for a nap.

A short time later, he wakes up refreshed but also needy. He crawls out of the bag and looks for some grass or a bush. He can't find any but sees what seems to be an acceptable spot under Ali's desk. In the dark, he circles, hunches, squirts, oozes, and eliminates the remains of all that rich food on the floor. Then, scooting along the floor to clean himself, he spreads the mess. Ali sits right above it. He sniffs and makes a face.

"Omar, did you just fart?"

He had, but it was a silent one. Omar lies—"No, I didn't"—and tries to sound offended.

"Well, I smell something really bad, and I know it wasn't me."

Ali has no choice but to put up with his brother, especially now in the final hours.

Soon the sheik will be released, and we can complete the mission. Then I'll be free of this annoyance. He enjoys a moment of rapture—the thought of what it will be like to be free of Omar. That is, until a frightening thought occurs to him.

What if Omar and I are sent to the same place in heaven?

To Ali, that's punishment. He gets down on his knees and prays for a fair and just reward. Leaning forward to rest his hands on the floor, he feels something moist and squishy. Somebody must have spilled something.

His prayer finished, he stands and wipes his hands with a paper towel from the desk. But the odor is still there.

That Omar! Allah forgive me for murderous thoughts about my brother.

YoYo continues to prowl through the lobby. He goes to the windows and peers out. Nothing holds his interest, so he wanders down the east hall. A bank of elevators separates it from the west hall. In the dark, he glimpses a gold mine of items fascinating to a dog. A discarded letter crunched up in a ball; a shiny object—a tube of lipstick that's good for rolling and chasing; an empty milk carton; and a half-eaten Twinkie. Before he can check them out, it happens—again—right in the middle of the hallway. It can't be stopped. He hunches, circles, squeezes, and finishes by scratching the territory. The lipstick tube gets caught in the mix. It careens down the hall and bounces several times before it rolls to a stop.

Omar looks up at the sound, but Ali is talking to Abdul. Reluctant to interrupt his brother, Omar decides to investigate and mumbles to himself in that foreign language. I don't need a translation. I know what he thinks as he walks into the dark hallway.

It's better if I do this by myself and not bother Ali. I don't want to get scolded again if I imagined the noise. No one can get into the hallway. We would know if anyone tried.

Something scoots past him.

He sees it again.

A rat!

Still limping from his fall, he chases after it. His foot lands on the lipstick tube. The tube rolls, and Omar falls, landing hard on his back. His legs shoot up into the air. Barely conscious, he is aware of a small dog who emerges from the darkness and trots over. Its nose goes sniff, sniff, sniff, all over Omar's body.

A dog, the dirtiest of creatures, has defiled me.

YoYo also has thoughts about the scents he's picking up.

Boy, this guy overloads on garlic.

Omar stands and limps after the dog.

I will capture it and take it to Ali. He will know what to do, and he'll be pleased with me. I'll show him I can do something right.

The dog runs down the hall. In the dark, I can see what's about to happen. But Omar can't, and you may be sure I wouldn't warn him if I could. Sure enough, his feet hit something wet and slippery. Legs fly in the air. His head lands with a loud thump. I do believe this time he is knocked out, so we wait. YoYo watches patiently, and I rest on a fire alarm until Omar regains consciousness.

He opens his eyes and looks around. He realizes that he is lying in something moist and squishy. He squirms, and the smell hits him. He cries, "It's the dog" and faints.

A little later, he wakes. Now his vision is hazy, and he is confused.

What happened? Where am I? Oh, I know. We got the sheik released in Nimbaba. Our mission was a success. So we detonated our bombs!

There is a loud sigh.

Well, blowing myself up wasn't as bad as I expected.

He looks around. He expects to see heaven. Instead, the same small dog sniffs his face. He feels the stuff beneath him, inhales the bad smell, and slowly his eyes close as he drifts away. His final thought: *So this … this is heaven? I knew it wasn't worth it.*

Isn't that a crock? We say the path to hell is paved with good intentions. Thank you, Omar. You just showed us that the path to hell is also paved with bad intentions. So the rule is modified from *Do No Harm* to—*Don't Even Try*. I wonder if Hippocrates would approve of my version.

Ali is off the cell phone. Omar is missing. Ali knows his brother went down the hall and hopes it was to use the restroom. The annoying smell still lingers.

After some minutes, he calls, "Omar." No answer. "Omar, get over here."

Still no answer. Instead he hears a noise. It sounds like a bark, and it comes from the hall. There it is again. A dog. He draws a dagger from his belt. Ali likes the feeling of the razor-sharp edge and a chance to use it. He heads into the hall, determined to get rid of what he believes is a minor annoyance.

Outside the building, Sgt. Jackson reports: "YoYo barked. Twice. So the cat's out of the bag. Or the dog's out of the closet. Or …"

The team looks at him quizzically.

Lt. Anderson snaps, "This is no time for levity," and turns to Sgt. Cameron, who peers into his nightscope.

"What's going on?"

"No sign of activity. The west hall is empty."

"Well, YoYo is on the move. God help us."

"No," objects Holly. "God help YoYo." She sinks to her knees.

Chapter Ten

Ali enters the hall with long strides, the kind of movement that sets off YoYo's alarm. He sits up like a meerkat to get a better look at this figure moving toward him. A thin shaft of light from the windows illuminates him.

Maybe it's Holly, and she's come to take me out of here. His nostrils wiggle and flare out to pull the scent in.

Ali stops when he sees YoYo. It's no exaggeration to say he doesn't appreciate how cute YoYo looks. He fingers the blade and mumbles loud enough for both YoYo and me to hear his threat.

"Big dog or little—no difference to me. I will take care of it."

Coolly staring Ali down, YoYo answers, *Oh yeah?* Yes, his *rrooorruuuff ... rrooorrruuufff*s definitely have attitude. These are not ordinary barks. Nature has given him the ability to amplify his barks to an obnoxious, deafening level. The intent is to make the enemy think he's large and dangerous, not a teeny-weeny terrier, and to scare the living daylights out of Ali. I've heard people say that their tiny dog acts like he thinks he's a big dog. No, that's not how it works. Your dog knows he's small. He wants you to think he's big. Amplification is one more tool in YoYo's arsenal, and he uses it on Ali.

Ali may not be scared, but he does have an uneasy feeling.

There's something familiar about that dog. Have I seen it before? Yes, I remember it now.

"Omar, where are you? Something strange is going on. That same demon dog from the park is in here. Is this an omen? Is something evil trying to wreck our holy mission?"

Sorry, but Omar can't answer. He's in another place now. Interesting that he calls YoYo "Demon Dog." Reminds me of a poem. I'll just say it's by "Anonymous."

> Demons are said to be fallen angels.
> Some of them are furry and bark.
> So what's in a name
> That which we call a rose
> By any other name would smell as sweet.
> That which we call a demon
> Could be a dog doing its job.

I admit to nothing.

The barks end when YoYo goes on the offensive. He streaks for Ali's ankle, bites, and retreats to his meerkat position, exhaling through his nostrils. It's a loud snort: *Hhhuuuffff!* People tend to think of dogs as just barking, but they do make a lot of sounds with their noses, including whines, grunts, and groans.

Ali counterattacks. He swings the dagger at YoYo, who speeds around him and bites the other ankle. Ali stomps his foot in anger. Uh-oh. I wonder what's going to happen now. That's the signal to play the "Stomp" game.

YoYo picks up the cue. He's ready to play. With *HehHehHehHeh*s, he circles Ali several times, moving closer to him. Ali swings the dagger. It hits YoYo's back, making a bloody streak. I belt out a silent scream, but YoYo is confused.

What the ... does the ... think he's doing! (Tsk tsk tsk, YoYo. I can't put those words in the report. Remember where it's going.) *That's not part of the Stomp game that Holly and I play. Okay, buddy, all bets are off. Now it's personal. Between you and me.*

He propels himself faster, with louder *Heh ... Heh ... Heh*s. All systems are in high gear to plot a strategy to outwit, outplay, and outmaneuver this guy. Ali is poised to stab him again, but YoYo takes off down the dark hall. Now that I think about it, his *Heh Heh Heh*s had a slightly different sound from the *HehHehHeh*s that I previously translated as *HaHaHa*s.

Could the vowel have been an *o*? Like "HoHoHo?" Or, "You think you've got me, but we'll see about that." What's Demon Dog up to?

Ali runs full speed after YoYo. He trips over something in the middle of the hallway and screams, "Aiiiiihhhhhh." I omit the cursing that follows. In the dark, he fumbles with the object he tripped on. His hands discover a leg. Then another leg, an arm, and finally the unmistakably familiar round bulge of a stomach.

"Omar, Omar, speak to me. Omar, Omar, what did you do? Why did you do this?"

Now I do feel sorry for Omar. Even dead, Ali castigates him. Can't say I didn't see it. Call it unbrotherly love.

"Omar, my beloved little brother, I dedicate myself—I will kill the evil dog that did this to you. Even though you failed me when I needed you, I will avenge your death."

Wow! Talk about ambivalence.

Ali plots a strategy for revenge. Instead of charging the dog, he intends to stalk it, moving slowly until he is close enough to lunge at it and drive the blade in. He remembers the oath he made in the park: *If ever I see you again, little dog, I will strangle you. I will put my knife into your foul, dirty little body and twist it. I will cut out your tongue. I will chop off your head. I cut you now, and I will finish the job.*

YoYo is not concerned. He's distracted by a package he has stumbled onto. It looks like the Twinkie he enjoyed so much. But this is a granola bar. In seconds, little teeth tear the wrapper open, and he happily munches as Ali moves in for the kill. I don't really need any celestial capabilities to know what's going to happen. Between Ali and YoYo is the same pile of poop that Omar skidded on. Yup, there goes Ali. He skids and falls backward into the mess. His head, jacket, and pants are mired in the foul odor he smelled at the desk. He knows.

"It's the cursed dog. Oh, why did I blame you, Omar. My poor, sweet brother. I wish you were here to help me now."

Ali tries to sit up, but it's too painful. He rages on with every curse he has ever heard. Certainly more than I have ever heard—and I omit them from my report. Stealthily—this time on hands and knees—he approaches YoYo.

"I've got you now, devil dog. This will be easy," he shouts.

For all his cunning, Ali is about to make another mistake. If he had lain quietly, YoYo would have continued munching on the granola bar, enjoying it. He would have ignored Ali, but that shouting was a trigger. YoYo may not have understood the curses, but volume is threatening to a little dog. When YoYo is threatened, we know he goes into action. A surprise attack is accompanied by deadly trilling sounds. *Eeeeee … Eeeeee … Eeeeee.* He darts straight for Ali's face. He literally flies in and out and around Ali's head, skillfully avoiding the dagger. Each circle gets him closer to Ali who, for the first time, is scared. He rolls onto his back to protect his face, and his arms flail wildly as if he fights a swarm of killer bees. YoYo detours in to bite his nose, then again chomps on his chin. Ali feels blood run down his face. He puts a hand up to check the damage. That allows YoYo to strike the other hand. The one with the dagger. He bites it. His teeth sink into Ali's wrist. He hits an artery. Blood spurts out. Ali drops the dagger to apply pressure and stop the bleeding. This is the wrist that wears the detonator. He takes it off and sets it beside him. He will need it to complete his mission. He looks at his watch. In thirty minutes, the plane will land, and the sheik will be released.

I don't need to bother with this dog anymore. Why should I? I will take it with me when I detonate the bomb. The blast will blow the fur off its ugly body. The agonizing death it deserves. And it's not going to my heaven. It's to the Underworld for filthy dogs.

Satisfied with the sentence he has imposed on YoYo, Ali settles back to wait for Abdul to call with the message that the sheik is free.

There have been many times that I wished I could communicate with humans instead of observing and reporting, but never more than now. If only Ali knew the paradise that awaits dogs, he would prefer going there instead of to … well … we know where he's going.

For sure, YoYo won this round, but, again, he's lost interest in Ali. He heads for the lobby and then into the west hall. Nose to the wall, site of his previous markings, he sniffs his way back to the vent where he entered and searches for a way to get into it, like a doggy door. He doesn't find one. What he does find is quite interesting and worth checking out.

Outside, Sgt. Jackson has listened to what is happening in the building. He reports, "Someone screamed, 'It's the cursed dog.' There's a lot of yelling going on." He pauses for a long moment. "Now there's silence. Not a sound in there."

They wonder what that silence means? Were the terrorists subdued? Is YoYo okay? They have no way of knowing. They realize that they bought into a crapshoot.

"What about YoYo?" Holly cries. "I want to know about YoYo."

"It's too risky to go in now."

But the lieutenant knows time is running out. The plane will land in Nimbaba in twenty-five minutes, and the sheik will be released. If the men inside are still functional, they will detonate the bombs. The sweat that pours down his face in the cool evening belies his calm exterior. His men know him, but Holly doesn't, and she argues that it's time to go in and save YoYo.

"Wait a minute. I thought I just saw something."

"What is it?"

Sgt. Cameron has his face buried in the viewer. "Damn! Now I can't see anything. I can't see a damn thing. It's totally black."

Sorry. I let that one slide, and I still don't know how to delete. Perhaps the Committee could think of it as something that holds water?

"What's the problem?"

"I don't know. It worked fine a minute ago. I'll try adjusting it again." He fiddles with the focus and mutters over and over, "What is it? What is it?"

Lt. Anderson demands to know. "Well, what is it?"

His face still buried in the viewer, Sgt. Cameron exclaims, "Chrissake! *Chrissake!*"

Please note again that there is no word substitution. There is confusion over the meaning of the word, whether it is a curse or a prayer, especially since the item of interest that YoYo discovered in the hall was Sgt. Cameron's nightscope. It has familiar scents, so when he stood on hind legs to examine the object, he leaned into it and came eye-to-eye with Sgt. Cameron. It's the last thing I expected—YoYo and the sergeant—eyeball-to-eyeball. I hope the Committee is watching. And that they have a sense of humor.

"I see an eye," the sergeant reports.

The team exchanges looks, and they all simultaneously mouth, "YoYo."

Holly peers into the viewer. One dark eye with a golden fringe.

"Yes, it's YoYo. Thank God! It's YoYo." She takes a deep breath of relief and leans against the building.

"Gentlemen, I believe YoYo has done everything he can. Now it's up to you. I want my dog back. In one piece."

They agree. It's time for their move. Lt. Anderson reports the situation to the center where everyone is waiting, counting the minutes they have left to stop the detonation. Captain MacDonald nervously drums his fingers on the table. He realizes there is more at stake here than his winning an election.

Did the pooch do it, or didn't he? If the SWAT teams can't get into the building before the bombs are detonated ...

It's a little late for you to realize that, Captain.

John knows that it's now or never and orders the lieutenant to proceed with their plan. The lieutenant tells his men, "You know what we have to do. We must stop them before they detonate either of the bombs. A second can make the difference."

They understand and nod in agreement.

Sgt. Gonzales moves to the side window of the west lobby, places an explosive against the window, and moves back. It explodes with a loud blast, and glass flies in all directions. The teams race through and get inside the building. Alarms scream. The hostages on the sixth floor scream and drop under desks for safety, terrified that the end is coming. At the same time, they hope it's the start of a rescue operation. The guards stand and take positions by the doors.

The blast didn't affect me because I saw it coming, but it frightened poor YoYo and probably hurt his ears. He scoots down the west hall, ears back, tail between his legs, and through the lobby to the east hall where Ali lies, still bleeding, but conscious and wailing.

"They're coming in. My mission failed. Oh, no, no, no. It's not time.

The sheik's not free yet." He contemplates his options. *If they capture me, I can't detonate the bomb. That gets them off the hook … and the sheik will go back to prison. On the other hand, if I do detonate the bomb now, before the sheik is free, I've lost my leverage. They don't need to free the sheik. Either way, the fact is, whether I detonate or not, the plane isn't going to land in Nimbaba. It will turn around and go back to America. I must decide what I should do right now. People are in the building.*

So Ali, we come to the same conclusion. For you, it's a lose-lose situation. But there's still a joker in the deck. YoYo.

Ali prays. "Allah, forgive me, for I have lost this battle. I cannot free the sheik. There's only one thing left for me—I can avenge him with this bomb. In your name, I will do it now."

He struggles to sit up, unwilling to enter heaven lying on his back in a pile of dog excrement. YoYo watches with interest. Ali stretches to reach a … a toy. That's what the detonator looks like to him—a metal gadget with some plastic.

Hey, that looks like one of my toys. Last time I saw it, it was under the bed. So how did it get in here? Anyway, now I've got something to play with. It's gotten deadly serious in here, and I need some relief.

He dives in and snatches the detonator away from Ali. "No," Ali screams as YoYo scampers off with it held between his teeth. Loosely, I hope.

Lights shine down the hall and black-clad figures rush into the hallway. One runs to Omar's body, sidesteps the mess, and removes the detonator still clutched in Omar's hand.

Others rush down the hall to Ali. They quickly check him and call out, "Detonator's missing."

Lt. Anderson shines his light in Ali's face, demanding, "Where's the detonator? *Where's the detonator?* You might as well tell us. Your plan failed. Your sheik is going back to prison."

Ali laughs and leans back. It's a sinister laugh.

Someone says, "Take a look at this."

A light shines up the hall and onto YoYo. He looks back at them, as surprised as they are. His coat is blood-smeared and sprinkled with shards of glass.

"What's that in his mouth?" someone asks.

There's a hesitation before we hear an answer. "I do believe it's a detonator."

YoYo is confused. He was all set to play with the detonator.

Who are these guys? Should I attack them? Hey, maybe they'll play with me. I'll give them a chance.

He drops the toy, the signal for the game to start.

Sgt. Jackson steps forward. "Maybe I can get it."

YoYo moves like lightning, snaps up the detonator, and scoots down the hall. He stops, waiting for them to give chase. The detonator falls from his mouth, clanging as it hits the floor, and bouncing a couple of times. The men freeze. Too bad they don't know the game. *Come on. Stomp, so I can run in circles.*

Sgt. Jackson is sweating now, but he tries again. "Nice little doggie, come on, good boy, let me have it." He follows YoYo down the hall and reaches for the detonator. But YoYo again scoops it up and runs two quick circles around him. Then he drops it and waits for the sergeant to stomp. If only they knew the rules, but the lieutenant has an ace to play.

"Get Holly in here. Fast," he commands.

Team members rush outside to where Holly is pacing nervously. Leading her into the building, they explain the situation to her, cautioning her to move slowly.

"The device is sensitive. One of YoYo's teeth could penetrate and set it off. We can't have him drop it again. It could trigger detonation."

A trembling Holly turns away in horror when they pass Omar's body. It's the first violence she's been exposed to. There's another shock when they pass Ali, lying in blood. Now she realizes what YoYo has gone through. This bloodletting, this killing, was far beyond anything she could have imagined. YoYo, still guarding his toy, doesn't recognize Holly in that black outfit and hat. She calls softly, "YoYo, YoYo, where's my little YoYo?" Ears go upright at the sound. Nose wiggles for the scent of this newcomer.

It's her. It's her.

Tail racing, he picks up the detonator and flies into her arms. Everyone gasps.

"Careful," the lieutenant warns.

She cradles his beat-up body and whispers, "How's my little boy doggie? Oh, you've been hurt. Don't worry, sweetheart. We'll fix you up real good."

Gently stroking his head, she tries to take his "toy" out of his mouth. He hangs on to it. He wants her to play the game and tug it—try to take it away from him. But her nose is so close, so irresistibly close, he has to release the detonator into her hand so he can give that nose a good lick. Holly takes the device from him and gently hands it to the bomb squad.

While Holly comforts YoYo, stroking his body and planting kisses on his head, the explosives guy, Jimmy Steffan, searches Ali. He mocks him. "Pheuuuu. What did you do here, fella? Shame on you."

Amazing that Jimmy kept his sense of humor.

"Don't you guys know how to use the restroom?"

Ali curses at him in two languages while a medic puts a tourniquet on his arm. My, my. Ali's extensive reservoir of curses continues as Jimmy handcuffs him. It's over, and now there is no doubt. YoYo won this round.

The team continues to search the building for the mininukes. They find the two suitcases in a restroom and carefully move them outside, where they go into a huge containment vessel that has a high-impact steel chamber. Now the city is safe. And YoYo survives to continue his evolutionary march into communicating with words. Or reasonable facsimiles thereof.

I'm getting a message. Those of us on missions get these transmissions. They're like CNN newsbreaks. Except they require no antennae, no satellites; no currents are needed. You could call it *knowing* because it's beyond language. Actually, it replaces language, tapping into what is needed to know, what must be known, what can be known—ultimate intelligence, beyond human comprehension.

The transmission I'm getting comes from deep inside a cave. I watch the leader receive news of the failed mission. He nods impassively and instructs his followers, "Send in the next team."

Oh dear. I'm afraid this means more terrorists on the way. I hope they won't be another add-on to this mission. Both YoYo and I have had enough of them. To be honest, if I had a choice, I'd prefer an ordinary bank robber any day. Unless the robbers switch from guns to nukes.

The transmission ends on that note so I turn my attention back to the federal building where a man enters and introduces himself to Lt. Anderson. He says he's Hal Brocklehurst, regional director of the FBI. I think Hal is a funny guy—the way he looks around the building—making clucking sounds like a chicken. He strolls to Omar's body. His eyebrows go up when he spots Omar in the muck.

"Well, look at this—the first fat terrorist I've seen."

Fat? To me, he still looks twerpy.

Hal strolls to a handcuffed Ali, who lies in the same ooze. He scratches his head and chuckles, "We have DNA, fingerprints, wiretaps, lie detectors, surveillance, and you mean to tell me that"—he points at the dog poop—"is what took those guys down? Did we miss something—a new kind of weapon?"

"Yeah, it's called YoYo," Lt. Anderson laughs, pointing at the messes. "And using all your resources."

"Well, at least we know there's plenty of that available."

"You betcha. This world is full of it."

The team continues the search for more evidence. In the lobby, they discover the bag of supplies.

"It could be a booby trap."

Jimmy Steffan puts on his protective armor and mask. He thought he saw some movement in it, and approaches it cautiously. Slowly, he opens it and takes a long look inside. Everyone's nerves are still on edge. When they see Jimmy wiggle his head back and forth, peering at something, they move back. Jimmy could be right. It could be a threat, but why does he keep staring at it? What's going on with him? At last, Jimmy takes his helmet off, pulls the mask up, and calls, "C'mere guys. You gotta see this."

Sgts. Cameron and Jackson join him, and a moment later, there is laughter. Lots of it.

"What's so funny?" Lt. Anderson asks.

"Well, it's the most dangerous ... *mouse* ... I ever saw. Right now he is absolutely destroying someone's lunch. It looks like chicken, some stew and—what's that? Some dates for dessert?"

"Is that our mouse? We thought he was dead. That YoYo took him down."

"Well, this guy is totally alive unless he eats himself to death. But don't worry; I'll take care of him."

Sgt. Cameron lifts the mouse out of the bag. It squawks and protests, unwilling to give up the best meal it ever had.

"Too bad for the mouse," Sgt. Jackson announces. "Sarge is taking it home for Meow's dinner."

"Nope. Fair's fair. It did the job, so it deserves to live. Okay, Mouse. You can go free, but I warn you, you'd better stay away from Meow. Because I won't be there next time to save you."

They tease him: "Hey, Sarge, you getting soft?"

He ignores them and takes the mouse outside and sets it on the grass. But there's no ignoring YoYo, who is outside with Holly. First he smells the mouse. Then he sees it. It's an "Aha!" Whether it represents a game to him, or a worthy opponent, he acknowledges it with a single *Heh*. Maybe it was a hmmmpph. There is also a slim possibility that the mouse responded to YoYo with what I swear had to be a grin before it ran off into the park.

The federal building is secure. The hostages can be released. It's over. Holly cries because YoYo looks so sad, so beat up. But he is alive, and I'm grateful for that. A medic bandages the wound from Ali's dagger. It's a surface wound and doesn't need stitches.

The lieutenant attempts to console Holly with good news. "The pilot got the news as he approached the airport in Nimbaba. He pulled the nose up, got altitude, and turned the plane around. It's headed for home now. They'll refuel in midair. The sheik is still on board. He'll go back to prison." He pats YoYo's head.

"I don't know what you did in there, YoYo, but whatever it was, it worked. I didn't believe it was possible when we started, but maybe you had an angel helping you."

No. No way. I didn't do anything except observe and report. If the Committee did send help, they didn't tell me about it. As far as I know, he did it all by himself.

Holly is proud of YoYo but vows that she will never, ever, let him be used again. On the way back to the command center, she calls Ted and explains what happened. He says he's coming to get them right away. We hear the shock and relief in his hoarse voice.

This has been a tough time for Ted. He got her message that she was going to be a little late. He waited and waited and then began to worry. It wasn't just that she didn't come home—BoBo and YoYo were gone too. At nine o'clock he paced the floor. It wasn't like her to stay out. He didn't know what to think. At ten o'clock he began calling family and friends. No one knew where Holly was. He felt that something was wrong. Holly is the love of his life, and the dogs ... without them ...?

He turned off that thought and continued his vigil by the window until the phone rang, and he heard Holly's voice.

I'd forgotten how nice it is to be loved like that. When Holly and YoYo enter the command center, BoBo is there to greet them, wagging. It stops when he sniffs YoYo. Bobo's nose travels the length of YoYo's little body and lingers on the bloody bandage. YoYo is hurt. BoBo's ears go flat, and his tail points down in sympathy for his friend.

John Travis rises to greet her. He hands her a telephone.

"It's General Vandersal. He wants to speak to you."

Holly takes the phone.

"Mrs. Hancock, thank you for helping us. We don't know what YoYo did in there, but we do know the terrorists were stopped. You have an incredible animal. The president sends his thanks and appreciation. Operation Demon Dog was the first of its kind and probably will never be repeated. It was imaginative, creative, and, I must say, 100 percent effective. We didn't have a single casualty. This is without precedent."

The people in the crowded room watch Holly as she listens, nods in response, and mutters, "Thank you. Thank you."

Captain MacDonald pays close attention. For him, this could be a bonanza. Unexpected recognition from the attorney general? That would equal an endorsement. He positively glows with anticipation. *I'm going to be the next district attorney.* When it happens, he will know who was responsible. He smiles at YoYo and murmurs, "Poochie, poochie. You're okay."

General Vandersal continues: "I know the entire country would be grateful to you and YoYo if they knew what he did in that strange, dark building, all by himself. But, unfortunately, Mrs. Hancock, they will never know. Because we cannot tell them. Because the mission, Demon Dog, must be classified Top Secret. YoYo has to be classified Top Secret. If our enemies learned about him and the mission, YoYo's life, your family's lives, would be endangered. We can't allow that. I'm sure you understand the need to protect YoYo. Operation Demon Dog was the first of its kind and probably will never be repeated."

The general would be surprised if he knew what Holly is thinking.

Are you kidding me? Of course, YoYo has to be protected. So does my family. And I don't care if the country can't know about it. I would prefer that, actually, because I don't need any more publicity. I had all I ever wanted from the foiled bank robbery. So classify him any way you want, it doesn't matter, because I will never again let him be subjected to that.

"So, Mrs. Hancock, even though America doesn't know what YoYo accomplished, we know, and we honor him."

When she hangs up, John announces that an official statement from Washington will credit a new robot for the mission. "And, further, Operation Demon Dog is declared Top Secret."

Captain MacDonald's mouth drops open.

What? I must not have heard correctly. I think he said the mission has been declared Top Secret. No. No. That means no publicity, no recognition for YoYo, no recognition for my part in all of this. Demon Dog was all my idea, and I won't get any credit for its success—the credit that would have gotten me elected.

What can I say except foiled again, Captain, for the second time, but you get no sympathy from me.

John addresses the FBI agents, the SWAT teams, the bomb squads, and the police officers. "Each one of you did an outstanding job today. Your teamwork was excellent, your timing, perfect. You carried out every order in a professional and efficient manner. I congratulate you and thank you for a job exceedingly well done."

He stands next to YoYo. I'm surprised because this time YoYo doesn't object when John pats his head.

"But we all know who the hero is. Here he is, just a little dog, but in these five pounds is the most incredible spirit and courage. It's sad that our country will not adequately reward him or honor him for what he accomplished."

The group doesn't understand yet, and they question John.

"Demon Dog has been classified Top Secret. You know what that means. No word of this operation must ever get out. That we, we alone in this room, have the privilege of honoring him."

"YoYo, none of us here today will ever forget you and what you did for us, for our country, and we salute you."

They all stand to join John in the salute to the bandaged creature nestled in Holly's lap. John moves to pet YoYo. He stops and laughs, and I know why. Now maybe YoYo was sleepy. Or maybe it was a twitch. But I saw it, and I'll call it as I saw it. And I'm not at all surprised that YoYo winked at John. It confirms what I suspected. YoYo knew what was going on all along. To him, it was all in a day's work.

But John can't believe it. "Do you know what YoYo just did? He winked at me. The dog winked at me."

YoYo, you are a little devil!

The laughter that follows is just what everyone in the room needs to relieve the pressure and stress that came with risking everything on a little dog. Now they can relax and celebrate. Me too. I feel so good, I'm going to flip out, cut loose, and do cartwheels, somersaults. Ouch! Maybe I got a little too far out. Stubbed my toe on the moon. Almost got into orbit. Sometimes I forget how awesome these wings are.

Back to business. They line up to praise and pet YoYo. The depressed captain is last. He forces himself to join in the gaiety.

What a character that dog is. I'm not going to write him off yet, even if he is Top Secret. The election is still several months away. You never know what might happen.

What an optimist you are, Captain!

To YoYo, he says, "Hey, pardner, good work."

Well, poochie, maybe we'll get another chance to elect me district attorney.

He still hasn't learned. If he gets a chance, he'll try again.

"Poochie" responds with a message for the captain. His lips curl.

Teeth are bared. We hear *Geeefff*. He is doing better with those *g*'s. His jaw drops and, unbelievably, his tongue is behind his front teeth, forming a *lllaaawwwwff* sound. Yes. That is an *l*. He used his tongue to make the *l* sound without the benefit of the scalpel. He repeats it. *Geeefff lllaaawwwwff*.

The captain pulls his hand back, embarrassed, and hopes the others haven't noticed. But Holly has, and she smiles for the first time that day. Maybe she understands what YoYo is trying to say. I think I know.

Replace the *f*'s in *ggeeefff* with a *t*—the impossible *t*—and it's "get."

Change the *w* in *lllaaawwwwff* to an *s*. Remember, *s*'s are difficult too. That makes it *lllaaasssfff*.

I'll bet my—oops! What I mean to say is that I'm *sure* "*ggeeettt lllasssfff*" is "Get lost." Or a reasonable representation of the phrase. That's *two* words! A verb, an adjective, and an implied pronoun. Which makes a sentence. YoYo came through for us, but I almost blew it again.

This is major, groundbreaking progress that I am proud to report. Huh? What's that? Not satisfied yet? Well, what did you expect? Morgan Freeman reciting "Four score and seven years ago?"

Was it smart of me to talk back like that to the Committee? There may be a penalty. But I can use my reward to get around it. I'll wish that angels don't have to be angels 24/7.

The captain backs away as officers escort Ted into the control center. Oh my, what an emotional reunion they have. BoBo presses hard against Ted's leg, and YoYo protests that he is scrunched because Ted hugs Holly so tight. She laughs. "I'm okay, darling. We're all okay." They leave, headed for their car. I jump on the dashboard so I can observe YoYo. If there is another breakthrough, I don't want to miss it. But he doesn't seem ready to make his jaws work, so there's no chance he'll provide us with a summary—from his point of view. I know I should resist invading his mind, but I really want to hear his take on the events of the day.

They put me to a lot of trouble to get that good meal. I hope it doesn't set a precedent. The shish kebabs were good, but I would have settled for a turkey-jerky.

And I thought he was clever when he maneuvered around a lamppost.

Imagine what Fido's first conversation with his master will be like. There's more.

True, the running and excitement increased my pulse rate. Boosted the metabolism. Prevents clogged arteries. With my job, I have to look at the positive side. The high spot for me was—not seeing those guys go down, or even the feast. It was the mouse. Can't believe the crazy act he put on. Calisthenics, exhibitionism, overly self-confident, puffed up, swaggering. Kinda reminded me of Bruce Willis in the rerun of Die Hard *I watched with Holly. Nothing like that with the mice in my backyard. They're dullards who cave on the first toss.* [Yawn.] *Now I'm ready for a nap.*

Who knew?

He curls up in Holly's lap, while in the backseat, BoBo stares into my space. I wave. He nods. We're cool.

During the drive home, Holly tells Ted what she thinks happened to YoYo in the federal building. When she gets to the end, and the terrorists are defeated, Ted glances at YoYo with a half smile.

"Well, I guess you have to give the devil his due."

YoYo's head immediately comes up. He focuses on Ted with disdain. Lips curled, nose convulsed in spasm, he snarls his response: *Nnnnnnnooonnnooooowwww. No clichés, please.*

Okay, so *Nnnnnnoonnnooowwww* is a reasonable facsimile.

Holly ignores both of them and looks out the window at a car honking at them. A little boy hangs out the window, and waves at us. It's little Tommy Harper, and he's not crying anymore. He's going home with his father. My, he looks happy now that Dad's been released, along with the other hostages. Holly holds the still-snarling YoYo up to the window and tells him, "See that little boy. He got his daddy back."

YoYo looks out the window and wags his tail when he recognizes Tommy.

"You did that, YoYo. Now, wasn't that worthwhile?"

I expected the usual *aaafff*, or a *ruff*. What we heard was a *yyyyeeewwwfff*. The *y* sound is not new, and we're pretty sure now that the *wwww* sound is a substitute for an *s*. Well, what do you know. YoYo just said, *Yes*, or *Hey, I was just doing my job.*

That said, he curls into a ball on Holly's lap.

Please, I need my rest. Wake me when we get home.

Ted squeezes Holly's hand. That's easy. It's an "I love you." He kind of makes me nervous the way he keeps taking his eyes off the road to gaze at Holly while crooning, "I can't get along without you."

In conclusion, my dog has spoken on several occasions. He said several words and even formed a few sentences, providing incontrovertible evidence that evolution is progressing. The Committee will be pleased, as I am. Now that we are certain to hear more words from YoYo, it's time to think about the rewards the Committee offered. Which should I choose? I think my best bet is to go for a wish. But what should I wish for? Being with YoYo is the only thing I really want, and I can't have it. There must be something that would make me as happy as I am now.

On that optimistic note, I close today's report with a postscript.

When the officers escorted the hostages out of the building, one of them stopped to ask whether it was true that a small dog disarmed the terrorists. They had heard a rumor.

An officer paused for a moment and smiled before he responded. "And some people actually believe in the Loch Ness monster, Bigfoot, Sasquatch, and extraterrestrials."

Anyone up there smiling?

Chapter Eleven

Here we go again. I don't get it. The Committee has sent another variation on my mission. That's fine, but the problem is that, once again, it has nothing to do with dogs speaking. They know YoYo has recovered from the ordeal with the terrorists, so they think he's ready for another adventure. Poor YoYo. Perhaps he'll rebel this time and tell them … However, I admit that I'm ready for another dose of excitement. But I do wonder—were these detours always part of the plan? Is there a subplot? Reduce crime while waiting to hear words spoken by my dog? Do I get advantage rewards for the add-ons? A lot of questions, but no answers.

This one means getting involved in what cops call "a drug deal gone bad." Sounds far-fetched to me. However, if YoYo lives up to form, it's curtains for the main player in the new scenario, Hector Santos.

So far all I know is that Hector left Juarez, Mexico, last week. He trekked through the Chihuahua desert carrying a backpack containing eighty pounds of drugs. He was hungry and thirsty, had to dodge Border Patrol and ranchers' dogs, but he finally got to Tecate. He made the trip alone because he couldn't trust anyone with that big a shipment. Using phony papers, he bought a car for $600. A good investment, he thought, because they promised him a big bonus when he delivered. With the backpack stashed in the trunk, he headed west and stopped only to fill up on the outskirts of Los Angeles, where I join him. We're driving north into the Tres Los Rincones National Forest, the designated spot for delivery.

This mountain road has tight curves and is lined with rows of conifers. I will take the liberty of adding information on some of the interesting flora and fauna of this planet because selective transfers of some of the species to other galaxies could be beneficial to the universe. With the exception of humans, obviously.

The ponderosa pines are the tallest. I'll bet they're over one hundred feet. The view is like a postcard. We pass a group of knobcone pines with unique curled trunks. Each tree has several twisted tops like corkscrews. Next are the Jeffrey pines, with their straight trunks, evenly spread branches, and bark that smells like vanilla, lemon, and violets. If you could bottle that, it would outsell Chanel #5. Not one to miss an opportunity, I flip out to have a quick sniff. I'm really enjoying the scenery. It's kind of ironic. In my lifetime, I always wanted to take a trip to California. Now, after I've done the tour to Pluto, Mars, Lyra, and numerous galaxies, I finally get to LA.

Hector arrives early, pulls into the deserted parking lot, and turns off the engine. We wait. Moments later, headlights appear from the other end of the lot, and a car drives toward us. Hector is uneasy. They're early. They're never early. They always make a point of being on time; getting in and out fast is their method. It limits their exposure.

The driver pulls up next to us. It isn't Adolpho. The man in the passenger seat gets out and comes to our car. It isn't José. This is not the usual team. Hector doesn't know them, and I don't need to know these guys. They're bad news for Hector. Apprehensive, he keeps the door locked. I slip out to watch how this will play out. For sure, something's going to happen.

The driver calls, "Hey, Hector, Carlos sends his regards." Carlos is one of the Sinaloa cartel bosses.

"You got something for us?" the other man says. A relieved Hector clicks the doors open.

"In the trunk," he replies, getting out of his car. He resists asking about José and Adolpho. In this business, you don't mention names. Or ask questions.

Hector opens the trunk. He takes out the backpack and glances at the other car. The driver has a gun pointed at him. At first, he is surprised. Then it hits him—they're going to hijack the drugs. He pushes the backpack into the man standing next to him. The man falls. The driver fires his gun. The bullet tears through Hector's jacket. It penetrates his shoulder. The man pulls himself up. He unsheathes a wicked-looking knife, waves it at Hector, picks up the bag, and throws it into their car. Hector panics at losing the drugs. He moves toward them, but the driver fires again. Hector dives under his car. He needn't worry, because the hijackers drive away. They have what they want.

I begin my first report on this new mission with two questions.

The first is, what part will YoYo play in this drama as it unfolds? The second is, how will it unfold? It would help if I knew what to expect. Not that I can do anything about it. I am here to observe and report on any evolutionary progress dogs, specifically YoYo, have made in learning to speak. I digress to explain that's not as much of a reach as humans might think, considering that their own speech actually began with primitive sounds probably similar to the bark.

Those sounds were used as a defensive device to intimidate predators. Surely the first time a human screamed "Yeeoooowwwwwuuu" at a saber-toothed tiger, it stopped in its tracks. I can only imagine the grunts needed to scare a flying reptile. Did they survive an attack from a woolly mammoth with an angry shout that meant in no uncertain terms, "Leave the reservation?" Evolution took those sounds up a notch, and humans began to use them to communicate with each other. Grunts and snarls gave way to "Hello, how are you?" but slowly, over thousands of years.

I want to emphasize, and it is generally acknowledged, that all the sounds dogs make do attempt to communicate. They carry a message. My mission is based on the belief that, in time, though we don't know how long it will take, their barks will also evolve into a language similar to the ones humans use, employing the same vowels and consonants. It probably won't sound the same, but at least it will be something we can understand better than *wooofff, wooofff*.

To review, YoYo has shown progress in forming some of the difficult consonants such as *y* and *g*. He has trouble with *s*'s, and *t* is just about impossible, although he did link two separate words to form a sentence. Admittedly, I took some liberties in substituting a few consonants. I do, however, warn that our expectations shouldn't be too high. The reality is that the Fidos of the world, when they do speak, will not sound like Dirty Harry saying, "Make my day," or Vivien Leigh trilling, "I'll think about that tomorrow."

What will the sound be? I suspect it will be something like a combination of ET and Donald Duck. On steroids. We understood them, didn't we? Excuse me. I mean, didn't they? Because I'm in another category now. And, I might add, happy to be here. Life was never as exciting or challenging as this evolving mission that took me from the Dimension and now to Hector and his problems.

Those problems didn't end when the car drove away. They begin anew as a familiar car drives into the lot. This time it's the real team. Hector knows them well. He has delivered to José and Adolpho many times. They are tough and mean and expect the drugs or else. When the headlights hit him, he wallows in self-pity for a moment, thinking what they will do to him when they find out he doesn't have the drugs. He snaps out of it and runs for his life.

His short legs fly through a series of parking lots. Breathless, he stops to look back. The car follows him. José runs beside it. Hector doesn't know what to do. Should he try to explain to them that he arrived with the drugs, but they were hijacked? The answer comes quickly with another question: are you kidding? He continues to run. He reaches a community next to the park and races through rows of houses. The men are close behind him. Exhausted, sweating, and terrified, Hector is determined to escape somehow.

He opens the gate of a small house and goes to the garage. He's in luck. It's unlocked. Inside, the walls are lined with cabinets. One looks large. He considers whether he can hide in it. He tries to crawl in, head first. His feet stick out; his body is too long. Tumbling out, he starts over. This time legs and feet go in first. But his ample body hangs out. He leans into the cabinet and puts his head between his knees. That has to be uncomfortable, but if two killers were after me, I'd consider refuge in a matchbox. He adjusts his position and hits his head, groans, and backs out. I observe these calisthenics from the outside. No way am I going to join him in there and watch him squeeze his bulk like an accordion.

Hector doesn't give up and backs his body in, lies flat, pulls a leg in, and tucks it under his butt. He folds his other leg under an armpit. I used to do something like that in yoga. I did it to relax. Hector can't relax because the garage door is opening. A car engine starts. He opens the door a sliver to peek. The car backs out and drives away, but he glimpses another car driving slowly through the alley.

It's their car. They're still looking for me. It'll be light soon. Then I'll escape.

He's a human knot, but to survive, he sticks it out. Even Buddha would be impressed.

Chapter Twelve

New instructions arrive. Just when I started to relax with Hector safe in the cabinet, I have to change locations.

Not far away, Mike O'Reilly's alarm goes off. It's 5:30 a.m.—time to shave, shower, get breakfast, and drive to Forest Hills Elementary School, where he picks up the school bus and starts his route. Mike loves this job and the kids. He retired from the US Postal Service with a decent pension. This is a part-time job. And he's good at it. He listens sympathetically when the fourth- and fifth-graders complain about homework and mean teachers. He counsels second- and third-graders to pay attention while the kindergarten and first-graders giggle and play. With the pre-Ks, Mike is grateful to be entrusted with them. He'd give his life to protect them.

I suspect this mission is about to take an interesting turn, so I settle on the dashboard to keep Mike company.

Mike's route consists of estates and more modest homes that back up to the same heavily wooded national forest that Hector and the cartel use for a drop-off. That could be a coincidence or …?

It's getting light now, and we stop to let morning joggers pass. A woman with a big black Labrador and a tiny terrier crosses in front of the bus, the terrier barking and straining at the leash to catch up to the joggers. They think he's cute and laugh at him. The woman's command to sit is ignored, although the Lab obeys. The terrier emits constant *woof … woof … woof*s.

Mike mumbles to himself, "There's something familiar about that woman."

Did I see her on television? Something about a dog. That's it. Her dog foiled a bank robbery. The mayor and police department gave him all kinds of medals. But it couldn't be that wimpy dog. She must have gotten another one.

The dog is indeed YoYo. That's no coincidence, I'm sure. Well, I'm not so sure. I still don't know how this hand we've been dealt will play out. The way I always played the game, you had to have all the cards.

I'd like to tell YoYo to stop the yapping and behave, but I can't. Instead, I flow through the bus to him, rumple through his short fur, and circle his tummy. He likes it—it feels good. I flop inside his ear, tickling him. Will he say something? Come on, YoYo. This is your chance. You could help me qualify for that reward. He does. It's a *Whaaaff? … Whaaaff?* That could be a word.

I have a routine now for identifying words. I run through all the consonants. Something interesting turns up when I get to a *t*. Does it fit anywhere in W*haaaffff?* Yup! If the *f*'s in *whaaaff* become a *t*, he's saying, "Whaaatt? Whaaatt?" Like "What bit me?" I want to tell him, "It's just me, YoYo, pushing you down the road to expressing yourself in English."

He doesn't have a clue about what's going on. That makes two of us. So I hop back through the bus. Mike puts it in gear and drives to the first stop.

Kevin Cohen waits at the gated driveway of an impressive estate with manicured lawns and extensive gardens. Kevin expects to follow in the footsteps of his scientist father, who made a fortune with clever inventions. Kevin wears contact lenses now—the big horn-rims discarded—and the girls have taken notice. He is a handsome boy. Polite too. Says "Good morning" to Mike when he gets on the bus and moves to the back row. He opens one of the big books he carries and buries his face in it. An incurable snoop, I jump into the pages. Ugh! It's algebra. I make a hasty exit. Never did like it. Flunked it twice. It was a miracle when my checkbook balanced. At least I don't have to worry about that anymore.

The next stop is another estate. Sibel and Mabel Champion, twins dressed in identical outfits, hold hands at the gate. Their stretch yellow tunics over white T's, with white leggings and black boots look like their mom shops on Rodeo Drive in Beverly Hills. As we pull up, a stretch limo drives out, and the girls wave good-bye to their parents, who are taking another extended trip. They love to travel and leave the twins in the care of Lupe, their nanny. The twins hang on to Lupe's hand until they board the bus. Immediately, they begin one of their nonstop conversations with each other. I think they're more than identical twins. Their every move, gesture, and expression mirrors the other's. Always in sync. If they don't seem to have any friends, it's because they don't need any. They have each other.

Driving the next three blocks is like going to another town. The mansions and gated estates are gone, replaced with small, mostly run-down houses. Lawns are dead or dying and littered with bicycles, kites, baseball bats, and strollers. Mike stops in the middle of the block to pick up kids from five homes, but only an elderly woman waits.

"All the kids are sick with the flu," she tells Mike.

"Hope they feel better soon." But he worries that the whole school might get the bug.

The Hansens are next. Fifth-grader Katy takes charge of her younger siblings, Tommy and Scotty, to make sure they're ready on time. They both have the same white-blond hair and freckles as Katy. Scandinavians. They pile into the bus with books and lunch bags. They prefer the lunches their mom puts together to the free lunches the school provides. Sometimes they get one of her homemade oatmeal-peanut butter-chocolate chip cookies. Considering that their school just hired a chef, it's a big compliment to mom's cooking.

Once aboard, Scotty and Tommy trade punches. I've always wondered why boys like to hit each other so much. Katy moves to the back row where Kevin sits. He glances up at her and blushes a deep red. She ignores him and takes a brush from her bag, nonchalantly running it through her shiny hair. Mike watches from the rearview mirror and smiles. He knows what's going on.

Our next pickup waits with her mother. Pre-K Christine MacDonald is such a pretty child. Her big eyes are an unusual turquoise that complements pink cheeks and red-blonde hair. She wears a trendy dress with a black-and-white-striped top, and a pink tutu skirt topped by a polka-dotted vest. Her leggings are black-and-white polka dots, and her shoes are pink Mary Janes. Her mom spends some time dressing her. She looks like a junior version of a *Vogue* model. Mike lifts Chrissie into the bus and sets her in the seat behind him. When her mother leans in to plant a kiss on her head, Chrissie cries, "Mama!" Mike is prepared for these occasions. He opens a bag by the dashboard.

"Chrissie, would you like to see Happy?" He offers her a toy dachshund, long and skinny, with short legs.

Tears stream down her face as she nods and cradles Happy in her arms.

"She's going to be okay," Mike tells her mother, closing the door. Mom watches the bus until it turns the corner before leaving for her part-time job. The job that helps pay the bills while Chrissie's father is in Afghanistan, serving in the Marines.

Last stop is the Williamses. Tall for her age, Vickie wears a bright-red sweater with jeans. Her dark hair is in neat dreadlocks. She's an exceptional student—always gets A's, sometimes A+—but you can't say that about her brother, Willie. He's quite a case ... makes the bus wait while he ties his shoelaces, drinks orange juice, searches for his homework and books. Runs back into the house for lunch money, his jacket, or hat. It irritates Mike because it makes them late. But Mike has to admit that Willie makes him laugh. Willie can make anyone laugh. Vickie says he stays up late to watch Leno, Letterman, and other comedians. Their mother has to roll him out of bed in the morning.

California has a law that a driver cannot leave a school bus with students in it, but this morning Mike is impatient. For the first time in five years, he breaks the rule. He leaves the bus running in park and walks to the open door.

"Hello. Here to pick up Willie."

Willie's mother answers. "Oh, Mike, this boy drives me crazy. It's a struggle to get him out of bed. He's getting dressed now. I'm getting his stuff together. Can't find his homework. Do you see a notebook on the kitchen table, Mike?"

Mike does. It's on the table littered with breakfast dishes. He takes it to her as Willie makes his dramatic entrance sliding across the waxed floor. He pulls on a shirt and gulps juice at the same time, scoots into the living room, finds his shoes by the TV, grabs the bundle from his mom, and flees.

"Bye, Ma."

"Willie Williams, you behave yourself today." His mom sinks into a worn chair, sighing, and says to Mike, "I don't know what to do with that boy. His teachers tell me he acts bad, makes trouble in class, gets sent to the principal's office. Don't know how many times I've had to go to school about him."

Mike's already late, but he takes a few precious minutes to console her. I'd do the same thing—if I could talk to humans. And he does it at exactly the same time that Hector peeks out of the cabinet. It's morning and the garage is filled with light. That's the signal for his departure from the garage and the torture he's endured.

I land on the windowsill and bask in the sunlight streaming through the window. It's been a busy morning. So much activity and more to come, I'm sure, so while I'm waiting, I'll relax a bit and watch the dust bunnies floating. The windows are dirty, but who washes garage windows?

The sounds of doors opening and closing and traffic on the street are encouraging to Hector. He tumbles out of the cabinet, but his limbs are numb. He can hardly stand. He knows he may have to run, so he stretches and paces the garage to get his circulation going. The neighborhood is quiet as he opens the garage door, and sneaks past the little house. He steps onto the sidewalk. A car stops on the next block. A man emerges from behind some bushes and goes to the car. It's José!

Hector ducks back. José didn't see him. Stealthily, he slinks down the street. A dog barks an alert. José nods at the driver and hurries toward the bark. All the neighborhood dogs get the message that there's an intruder and join the alarm. The car makes a U-turn and goes around the block. Hector breaks into a run and turns left at the corner. The car appears dead ahead of him. He turns right, and there's José. Hector opens a gate and runs through the yard to the alley. He darts through another gate to a street where, a few blocks away, a big yellow bus sits in front of a house—its motor idling, the doors open.

Inside the house, Mike consoles Mrs. Williams. "Willie is a good kid. Just rebellious. The best thing you can do is be patient with him. I know, because my son was impossible just like Willie."

My son was a lot worse.

"But he straightened out. Made valedictorian. Got a 3.8 average."

My son didn't make valedictorian, and he got a 3.4 average.

"Now he's a successful attorney."

Mine is a dentist.

All this is easy for us to tell her now. Especially easy for me, under my decidedly different circumstances. And a whole new perspective.

Outside, Vickie waits for Willie by the bus. A tiny terrier runs down the street. He stops to visit her. She pets him and notices he's missing his collar.

"Hi there, cutie. You are soooo cute. Who do you belong to? Where ya goin' in such a hurry?"

A barefoot Willie flies out of the house and into the bus. Vickie instructs the dog to go home and follows Willie. The dog doesn't obey. He follows her onto the bus and jumps onto the seat with Chrissie.

"Lookie!" she exclaims. "I have another dog."

Nobody pays any attention. After all, she is only a baby.

But the dog is YoYo, so whatever is going to happen will start soon because Hector is running down the street toward the bus. He jumps on it and closes the door. Stomping hard on the gas pedal, he drives off.

Mike and Mrs. Williams hear the bus and rush out of the house in time to see it roar down the street. Mike blames himself.

"Too much temptation for young boys. One of them decided to take the bus for a joyride," he tells Mrs. Williams.

A brutish-looking man cursing in a foreign language runs past them. A car pulls up next to the man, and he gets in. They speed off after the bus.

"Something's wrong." Mike takes out his cell phone and dials 911. "Maybe the kids didn't take it."

"Excuse me."

Mike turns, and there's Holly. It figures. She lost YoYo when he pulled out of his collar to chase a cat.

"Did you see my dog? He's a Yorkshire terrier, about this big."

"Ma'am, we didn't see your dog or any dog."

"You must have seen him. He came this way."

"Lady, I've got a more serious problem than a lost dog. Hello? Hello? I'm calling to report a stolen bus ... with nine kids on it ... I'm the bus driver."

Holly's head jerks around when she hears those words.

"Are you saying that someone took a bus with children on it?"

Mike ignores her. "It was headed for the 801. I'm at 1610 Forest Drive. Yes, I'll wait right here."

"Oh no." Holly takes out her cell phone to call her husband to tell him it may be happening again.

"YoYo loves kids. And kids always love YoYo. I think there's a chance he got on that bus with the children."

Mike snorts. "Well, if he is, it's too bad he's not a German shepherd. A dog like that would protect the kids."

I love her response.

"You don't know YoYo."

Chapter Thirteen

Within minutes of Mike's 911 call, squad cars arrive at the Williams residence. An order goes out on the police radio.

"Attention all units: nine children kidnapped on Forest Hills Elementary school bus. Repeat: nine children, ages four to eleven. All available units proceed north on Highway 801. Locate and apprehend yellow school bus No. 42, license ED 45012. Bus is followed by black Toyota. Occupants, two men. May be dangerous. Use extreme caution."

An Amber Alert has already been issued. Ten units head north on the 801 in pursuit; six Highway Patrol units will meet them. A helicopter is in the air. I drop into the station to observe what will be a massive operation. Even though they activate all their resources, there's one thing I wish I could tell them: until they find the bus, YoYo will do his best to protect those kids. But even if I could tell them, would they take me seriously? That's a rhetorical question. We know the answer.

Uh-oh. Guess who's in charge at the station? None other than the superambitious, frequently foiled Captain Michael MacDonald. He queries Detective Baker about a motive for the kidnapping.

"No, Cap. This doesn't feel like a kidnapping. That takes planning. This sounds like it was random … like the bus just happened to be idling in front of the house. But then, maybe you're right, and the rich kids are the target. There were at least three on the bus … no, I don't think so. It sounds to me more like someone saw the bus—it was just sitting there—as an opportunity. Maybe someone wanted to escape from those guys in the car."

"Right. That would make the driver the target and not the kids." Lt. Jimenez agrees. "I have an idea that drugs are involved. We know the cartels use the park for pickups. The runner doesn't deliver. Cartels don't like that. He runs, stumbles onto the bus, and drives away. But they're right behind him."

It's amazing the instincts some cops have.

"Worst case?" Detective Baker adds. "The guys catch up to the driver. We know what will happen to him. Which could mean the kids witness some violence. Maybe even murder."

The lieutenant frowns. "Good God! That means we have to tell hysterical parents not just that their kids are on a stolen bus, but that they're in the middle of a drug war."

"No," the captain corrects him. "We don't say anything about that now. Let's stay cool about this. Let's check with the park folks and see what they have on their security cameras."

The others know the captain has political aspirations. The whole department understands that his hopes of winning the election will be dashed if they don't find the kids—and fast.

Luck may be on your side this time, Captain, because YoYo is on that bus. And I'm betting on him.

Darn. I did it again. Oh well. I'll say it's just a figure of speech. Old habits are hard to break. It's all those visits to Vegas and the blackjack tables. "Bet two, double the bet, bet the pot," and pretty soon it's part of the vocabulary.

Parents rush to the school. Reporters and media trucks race to cover the story. Captain MacDonald heads for the school to meet with the families. He enters the auditorium filled with weeping mothers and stern-looking fathers. I anticipated his reaction to the scene, and he doesn't disappoint.

These are the people who can vote for me.

I know he can't help himself. He's worked hard and wants to move up.

Maybe this crisis will be the one that I can turn into an opportunity to gain votes.

He still smarts from being unjustly denied credit—he thinks—for the terrorist episode. He has a grudge against the attorney general for the Top Secret call and is even more antagonistic toward the mayor, who upstaged him at the award ceremony. The captain certainly is a candidate for anger management therapy.

"Ladies and gentlemen, I feel what you are feeling." He squeezes his eyes tight. "You should know that I will exert every effort, use every resource available to our city, county, and state to bring our children home, safe and sound. My children. Yes, I do consider each and every one of those nine children as one of my own."

I clap silently for a performance worthy of an Academy Award.

The reporters, eager to get the story, move close. It seems as if every TV channel, radio station, and national newspaper is represented here. A photographer aims a camera, and the captain starts to grin, then quickly switches to a grimace. Lt. Jimenez watches from the door with Detective Baker and groans.

"There he goes. Why does he have to do that? Why can't he be himself—just a da—[word sub] darn good cop?"

"He wants to be district attorney. The thing is, if he ran on his record, people would vote for him. Our crime rate is way down since he got the job."

After telling the audience to keep trying to contact the children on their cell phones and Blackberries, the captain turns the stage over to Lt. Jimenez to answer questions and heads for the exit. A woman with bright, red-blonde hair stands to get his attention.

"Grandpa, Chrissie is on the bus."

He stops. He couldn't have heard right.

Not Chrissie, please not Chrissie.

Chrissie is his four-year-old grandchild. The daughter of his son serving in Afghanistan, and the same four-year old who played with YoYo on the bus. Amy MacDonald sobs. Anguished sounds come from the captain. Some mothers join them, and fathers blink back tears.

Lt. Jimenez observes the scene from the stage.

"Well, I'll be a [omitted]. Our captain really does have a heart."

An officer waits for the captain to collect himself.

"Captain ..."

"Yes?"

"There's something you should know. I think you'd want to know."

"Okay."

"A woman was on the scene looking for a lost dog ... a little dog."

Wiping his eyes, the captain repeats, "A lost little dog?"

"Yes, sir. The woman said he chased a cat."

"A young, attractive woman?"

"Yes, sir."

"The dog's a Yorkshire terrier?" *Please say no.*

"Yes, sir. The woman thinks the dog might be on the bus with the children. I think you know her."

"Well, well, well. I believe I do. It sounds like my least favorite Poochie. You know what, Officer Blakely? We thought we could handle this situation. But we were wrong. Not if it's who I think it is on that bus. Get on the radio. Tell all units to prepare. Tell them we think YoYo's on board. They'll understand. Anything can happen."

You got that right, Captain.

Chapter Fourteen

The bus thunders down the street. It's Hector's only chance to get away from the people trying to kill him. He barely misses hitting José, who's still running on the street. José manages to dodge the bus and glances up at the driver. Hector wants to laugh at his expression, but he's distracted by the noise coming from the back of the bus.

He looks around to see what's going on.

Tommy and Scotty are still punching each other. Then they switch their attention to Willie. They tease him mercilessly while he tries to put on his shoes. Willie retaliates and punches Tommy. Scotty goes to the aid of his big brother and stomps on Willie's bare foot.

Willie hollers, "I'm gonna get you, freckle-face," and dives at Scotty. The three boys fall, wrestling on the floor of the bus.

Hector almost drives off the road.

"Tommy, Scotty, you stop that," big sister Katy warns. "Go sit down. I'm going to tell Ma about this."

Scotty, suddenly aware, shouts, "Hey, Mike is driving fast."

Tommy calls out, "Hey, Mike. You're gonna get a ticket."

"That's not Mike," Kevin informs them.

The children scrutinize the man driving the bus ... in the opposite direction from the school. Blood runs down his arm. He's a stranger.

Kevin closes his algebra book. "Carjacked. He carjacked the bus, us along with it."

But Hector's not worried. He had a brainstorm.

American kids! I'm saved. They wouldn't dare try anything with a school bus full of American kids.

Relaxed and confident that he escaped, he drives onto Highway 801. His peaceful solitude is interrupted by Sibel's and Mabel's screams—in perfect unison.

"The man in that car has a gun."

Scotty shouts, "Hey, they're shooting at us. Duck, everybody."

Hector looks out the side mirror.

It's them. How did they find me?

He floors the gas pedal as the highway begins its ascent into the mountains. Tall trees line the narrow road. It's the same road I took with Hector to deliver the drugs. But this time, I won't get to enjoy the scenery. He zigzags so the car can't pass him, tossing the children around. They scream in fear. The twins hug each other, sobbing. Chrissie thinks it's like a ride at Disneyland and screams with delight. Her new dog, YoYo, joins in the excitement. He barks short, snappy sounds. I hoped he was imitating Chrissie, but unfortunately her "Wheee, whhheeee, whhhheee's" don't sound anything like his *arf ... aaarf ... aaarfs.* The bus sputters from the strain of the uphill road. Hector isn't just agitated. He's scared.

If I don't make it up this hill, it's curtains for me.

Right, Hector, curtains, just like I predicted. Except there is an X factor. You may get lucky. YoYo's on board.

Chapter Fifteen

The bus coughs and sputters to the top and begins the long, curving descent from the mountain. The black Toyota is right behind it. I'm on the windshield of the bus, and now it's necessary to penetrate inside. A large tractor trailer is in front of us. Hector races to catch up to the truck. What's he doing? He's going to ram it. Oh! I see. He has a plan. Clever! Instead of using the brakes to slow down, he swings the big bus around the truck and onto the shoulder. He passes the truck, but too close to the trees for comfort. We go up on two wheels. All the children scream. Except Chrissie. She's still playing, having fun with her dogs.

The bus continues this mad run for what seems like fifty feet. Then, miraculously, it rights itself. Whew! That was close. Hector takes one hand off the wheel to make the sign of the cross. Really? I guess, under the circumstances, he got religion. People are funny the way they try at the last minute to save themselves. I should talk. I still don't know why I was allowed into the Dimension. In my lifetime, I never did that much good. But I never did anything bad, either. I tried to follow the oath: Do no harm. Maybe that counts.

The truck is now behind us. The sharp curves prevent the Toyota from passing, so it falls behind. Hector is encouraged. We pass a side road that heads into a dense forest. A second road is almost obscured by thick foliage. We pass a third.

I'll turn into the next one and take it as far as possible. They'll have to search the whole mountain for me.

However, Hector still has another problem: What to do about the screaming children and the dog. YoYo, his body rigid, stands next to the driver's seat, making intense, high-pitched *Rrroouufff … Rrroouufff*s. Ears and tail reach for the sky. The volume is up to 100 decibels, and it spikes at an ear-crunching 130 decibels. That volume increase is how nature intended him to handle an adversary such as Hector, who is several times his size. "You may think I'm small and helpless, but listen to this." His deafening, steady stream of *Rrroouufff*s is nature's design to discourage, annoy, antagonize, and intimidate—an effective formula for many animals. If I may paraphrase, it's "Get out of my face." It works. Hector resorts to talking to himself.

"If I can get out of this, if I make it back to San Miguel Allende, I swear I will never again be tempted to make an easy buck. I will be an angel."

I interject a "Hah!" Silent, of course.

He mumbles on. "I'll ask for my old job back. I promise I'll never go to sleep on the job again. To get my job back at the bus company, I'll buy a GPS, so I won't get lost anymore. If only I can find a way out of here alive."

He's so distracted, he almost misses the next road. It's lined with tall cottonwoods, and their wide-spreading branches form a canopy that makes it hard to see. The ground beneath the trees is covered in a thick growth of Hawthorne bushes. With a sharp turn, he swings the bus between the trees, and it bounces down the narrow, dark, unpaved road gouged with deep ruts. It twists and turns, going deeper into the woods. The children are jostled like rag dolls in open-mouthed terror. Even Chrissie protests, "I want my mama."

Ahead, Hector sees something glisten: Water—a lake. We head downward. The bus begins to slide. Hector struggles to steer as the bus ricochets between the trees. We hit water and then mud splashes up onto the windshield, making it hard for him to see. He hits the brakes, but his foot goes all the way to the floor. He can't stop the sliding bus. It speeds into waist-deep water and rocks precariously. Hector opens the doors, and water floods in. Without hesitation, he jumps out and heads to the shore. Looking back, he watches the bus wobble and turn on its side. Curious, he waits to see whether the children escape.

Luckily, the bus has turned so the door is out of the water. The panicked children slosh through the bus to get out. Vickie pulls Willie with her and turns back for the twins. Katy slides into the icy water and holds on to the bus while she urges her brothers to jump. Tommy leaps, but little Scotty hangs back. He's afraid the water is over his head.

"Come on, Scotty, climb on my back. I'll carry you," she tells him.

Instead, Kevin picks Scotty up and jumps into the water. He holds him up with one hand, and stretches the other to Katy. Gratefully, she clutches it. They wade to shore, sloshing in water-filled shoes, and collapse, shivering, in the mud. I hang out nearby in the rich, green branches of an incense cedar. Every branch is loaded with huge, fragrant pendant-shaped cones—a good candidate for exporting ... possibly to the newly discovered exoplanet—the one that orbits a red dwarf star. Scientists named it Gliese c. We call it Ditto because it's so much like Earth. Hah! I want to be there when future space travelers arrive. Boy, would they be surprised to find it stocked with cedars.

We've disturbed a flock of quail—hundreds fly out from the marsh as the children move inland to dry ground. Katy, the only one with a cell phone, reaches into a soaked pocket, and pulls out a muddy, dripping cell phone. She dials 911.

"It doesn't work. Why didn't I think of calling when I was on the bus?"

Vickie puts her hand to her mouth and exclaims, "My Blackberry!" She looks toward the bus, thinking of the hours of babysitting it took to buy it.

"Mine too," Kevin adds. "So we have no way to call for help."

They hear sirens, but they seem far away.

"We're stranded."

"How they gonna find us in here?"

A sound distracts them. It's coming from the bus, which is drifting farther out.

Yippp ... yippp ... yippp ... yyyyiiiipppp ... yippp ... yippp ... yippp.
Yippp ... yippp ... yippp ... yyyyiiiipppp ... yippp ... yippp ... yippp.

It's YoYo signaling an SOS. He stuck with Chrissie even when water flooded in, and he snagged a chunk of her tutu skirt, tugging until she crawled up on the dashboard. She's clinging to YoYo, and he's barking to get attention.

"Is that the dog Chrissie was talking about?"

"Chrissie?"

At last they realize that Chrissie is missing. YoYo did it again.

"Chrissie is still on the bus. We've got to get her!" Katy cries.

"Not possible. The bus is too far out now."

"You couldn't swim in that strong current, anyway."

"Hey, none of us can swim in that lake," Scotty adds.

Kevin studies the water. "Except that's not a lake. It's the Columbine River. Runs right through the park. Has lots of waterfalls—even rapids. Wait a second. I think I got an idea. We've got to save her. We can't let her go."

He surprises them. Me too. He's always been shy and quiet, and he is only eleven. They wait to hear what he has to say.

"Well, I'm not a great swimmer, but I've had lessons since I was a baby. I swim in the pool a lot, but I never swam in a river or even a lake." He pauses. "So—everyone—take off your clothes."

Kids, they never cease to surprise, but he does have a good idea. He kicks off his shoes, pulls off his sweater and shirt and unzips his jeans. The others blink in astonishment. I am amused.

"Come on, guys. Take off your shirts, your pants, we need them. We'll tie them together and make a line. I'll swim out to the bus with it and when I get there …"

"If you get there …" Willie is doubtful.

His annoyed sister elbows his ribs. "Shush, Willie. Don't be negative."

"I'll tie Chrissie to the line and you pull her in. I'll do my best to hold her up."

Vickie already has her new red sweater off. She unbuttons her jeans, steps out of them, and ties them together. All she has on is a white training bra and pink panties. Katy reluctantly takes her jeans and sweater off, eyeing Kevin as he takes her clothes and adds them to the line. The boys strip down to their jockey shorts. The twins watch with interest.

Sibel whispers to Mabel, "We have to take off our clothes."

"What'll we wear?"

"Nothin'," Sibel responds.

They look at each other, blink and nod, exchange information, and turn to the shivering group.

"If you promise not to look," they announce in unison.

The others have to laugh. They can't help themselves. Those twins are a kick.

Katy agrees: "It's a deal."

"And you, no peeking," the girls instruct Willie before they peel of their mud-splattered chic outfits.

Willie scratches his head and mutters under his breath, "Why would I wanna look at you two robots? Ya think you're Miss America?"

The girls, now down to their floral-printed little-girl bras with matching skimpy bikinis, hand their clothes to Katy. She adds their clothes to the line, but it's still short. Kevin notices a skinny tree floating nearby that must have been uprooted by the water. The boys wade in, grab the tree, and pull it to the shore. Kevin ties one end of the line around his waist, the other to the tree, which the others grip. While he wades into the cold water, I flip to the bus to watch his progress. Also to monitor YoYo's call for help. Was it really three dots and a dash?

Kevin begins with the smooth, even strokes of the Australian crawl, his face buried in the water. The strong current pulls him to the right so he switches to the breaststroke. Slowly he propels his body forward, then dog-paddles to the bus and climbs on it. The bus sinks deeper into the water. The group anxiously watches from the shore. Kevin disappears from view, and the bus sinks lower.

They yell, "Kevin, Kevin, get outta there."

Inside, the water covers the seats. A blue Chrissie hangs on to the steering wheel. Kevin picks her up and climbs out. The group on shore sees him holding Chrissie, who screams, "No!" Then they disappear from view. The bus continues to sink. They emerge again. This time Chrissie hangs onto one of her doggies. The real dog. YoYo.

Kevin holds Chrissie, and she holds YoYo as they plunge into the water. All three are submerged for a moment. Tommy yells, "Pull, pull!"

The kids grab the tree and pull backward until Chrissie pops up.

Her trendy dress is ballooned out with water, but she is still hanging on to YoYo. Using the lifeguard technique, Kevin holds Chrissie and swims the sidestroke. Katy and Vickie wade out to meet them and take Chrissie from him. They do their best to comfort the distressed child, taking off her dripping dress and soaked Mary Janes. She cries but clutches the tiny dog. The boys give Kevin a high five. They are all wet and cold, up to their ankles in mud, but safe for the moment. Relieved, I return to my perch on the fragrant cedar. Only now the branches are filled with squawking black crows, so I flip to a silver fir sapling, where I can hear the children consoling each other with optimism.

"They'll rescue us," they say over and over while the bus sinks to the bottom of the river.

Hector looks down from the ridge he climbed. He's relieved to see the bus sink and disappear.

Even if they drive down the road, there won't be no bus for them to see. That's a lucky break. I don't have to worry about them kids. They can take care of themselves.

He plods through the woods, avoiding the highway, every step painful from the wound in his shoulder, until he smells smoke.

Smoke? But fires aren't allowed in the park. What's going on?

The children had wrung out their clothes, taken off sodden shoes, and laid them on rocks to dry. They huddled together to stay warm. Then Willie picked up some dry twigs, announcing in a matter-of-fact voice: "Boy Scouts."

Sparks flew until he got a single flame going and a hearty fire followed. Scout counselors would have been proud of Willie. Now they sit next to the fire. Vickie says, "We're okay, but I'm worried about Chrissie." She holds the little dress close to the heat. "I want this to dry so I can put it back on her." Katy sets her cell phone on a nearby rock. She hopes it, too, will dry out and work again.

After one of their nonverbal exchanges, Sibel and Mabel announce, "We want our lunch now."

"Hey, me too," adds Scotty. He remembers the bags of sandwiches, apples, and cookies still on the bus.

"Willie, I so wish I had the peanut butter sandwiches Mom put in my bag. Why didn't I take them with me when we got off the bus?"

"Huh? Like maybe you were more concerned about getting out alive? But now that you mention food, I could go for one of Mom's pizzas. She makes the best ones—with tomatoes, olives, salami, mushrooms, onions, and lots of cheese."

"You forgot the garlic."

"Oh yeah. It's better with garlic and olive oil."

These kids salivate just thinking about that pizza. Except Chrissie.

"I want ice cream."

"Stop talking about food—it makes us hungrier. We've got to be patient. They'll find us. I promise." Katy is the most optimistic.

"I so hope you're right, Katy. I just wish I had my Blackberry."

They get an unexpected and uninvited visitor when Hector storms into their camp. He pushes them aside, stomps out their fire, and scatters the burning twigs. Now the X factor enters the fray. I mean the five-pound missile called YoYo that springs off Chrissie's lap. He plunges into Hector's big belly. His attack comes with a wild sound … *Wwoofffrrfff … wwooffrrfff …* More intense than previous woofs. YoYo bounces off Hector's belly and rebounds with another leap into that soft center. This time he growls. *Gggrrr … ggrrrr.* Love those *r*'s. But I wish they were the more difficult *t*'s. Hector staggers, falls backward, and lands in the hot embers of the fire. There is the smell of searing flesh.

"I'm on fire. Help! Help me. Owwwwoo."

He struggles to stand, but YoYo charges again. He leaps high. He likes that tummy as a target. It is a soft spot. Hector sidesteps to avoid him and turns his ankle on the embers. Another loud screech. Hysterical, he takes his fury out on the kids. Now he is a wild man. Katy tries to reason with him.

"Mister, we were just trying to get warm."

"I'll show ya how warm ya can get. You're gonna pay for this. I'm gonna get that dog. Ya like roast dog? That's what he'll be when I get my hands on him."

It seems to me we've heard that song before—from someone bigger than you, Hector. And he had a 9mm Glock. But he can't hear me, so he'll have to find out for himself.

If Katy is the group's optimist, Kevin is the protector. He picks up Chrissie and signals the others to follow. Katy pulls Tommy and Scotty with her. They run down the shore of the river and plow through the marsh. Vickie, still holding Chrissie's damp dress, follows with the twins, who hold hands and run in perfect step. Willie is the last. He's angry that his fire was smashed, but he doesn't want to tangle with a crazy guy. That's clear thinking, Willie. Go! Go! Go! Only my little YoYo stays behind to carry on the fight.

Hector can't catch him. YoYo runs fast in circles and snaps at every opportunity, snorting the jolly *Heh-heh-hehs* every time Hector says "ouch." He's having a good time. Rack up another round for Demon Dog while I follow the children. They run until they reach a shallow part of the river littered with big rocks. Tommy, Scotty, and Willie jump across on the rocks. Katy and Vickie lead the twins, and Kevin again carries Chrissie. They take refuge under a sixty-foot sycamore and look back at their former campsite, where the fight goes on. YoYo gets in lots of bites and enjoys every one.

"That's some dog you got there," Willie teases Chrissie. "Too bad he's not a Rottweiler or a Doberman." Whatever he is, she wants him back and begins to wail, "My doggie, my doggie."

Vickie says, "It's okay, honey. The doggie will be okay. Look, your dress is almost dry. Would you like to put it on?"

Chrissie is distracted by slipping the dress on. This time, there are no smart leggings or pink Mary Janes to complete the outfit.

Hector swats but can't connect with the artful dodger. He gives up and limps off into the woods. Defeat shows in a blob of pink flesh, exposed through scorched pants. Ouch! It looks like a bad burn.

The victorious YoYo puts his nose to work. Every dog has a GPS built into its nose. Butterflies and birds do too. The list of animals with such an efficient instrument is quite long. If you have ever wondered why a dog's nose is always wet, just watch YoYo. Watch him use his moist nose to detect the minuscule scented particles that dropped from the children. Those particles will lead him to them. The bloodhound is even more efficient. A stream of sticky drool drips from its nose, grabs those molecules, and pulls them up into the nose. Sniffed up, they zip along in a direct path to the brain for an ID. Those IDs are road signs that say, "This way. They went this way." It took humans a long time to play catch-up with the gadgets they use now.

"My cell phone. I left my cell phone on the rocks. I've got to go back to get it. It's our only hope."

"Wait," Kevin cautions Katy. He points to a black car that slides down the muddy road headed for Hector. Adolpho jumps out, and yells, "Hey, Hector. It's us. Just give us the package, and we're outta here."

Hector is surprised that they found him. He wishes he had the package to give to them. All his problems would be solved. But his only choice is to run again, and he takes off into the woods with Adolpho right behind him.

José gets out of the car and calls to his partner. "Adolpho, hold on. Wait a minute. Take a look! Do ya see what I see?" He points to the tree.

Adolpho looks up and sees the kids huddled beneath the sycamore. "So what, José? That's the kids from the bus."

"What I see is money."

"Yeah, money, and I'm goin' after Hector to get it."

"Peanuts."

"What's peanuts? A backpack full of stuff? Thousands of bucks ain't peanuts to me." He resumes the chase.

"Wait, amigo! Do ya know how much those kids are worth?"

"Whaddaya mean?"

"Think about it. Those kids are out here. Stranded. Nobody knows where they are. Nobody knows where *we* are. How many kids are there? I count … eight … nine kids. You see what I mean? We're never going to get a chance like this again. It could mean a million. We lucked out."

"Kidnapping?" Adolpho looks at the rock again. "Okay, but let's do it fast, so we can still get Hector and the pack. I know how much that's worth."

The children expect to see the men go after Hector. But when they keep looking at them, Katy and Kevin exchange looks. You would never guess that only hours before, strange new feelings made them self-conscious and uncomfortable. Now they are a team. When they see the men abandon the chase for Hector and head toward them, they know that now *they* are the hunted.

Kevin yells, "Follow me." This time Tommy picks up Chrissie, and they run barefoot into the woods behind them. Only Katy stays behind. Kevin stops to wait for her.

"Go ahead, Kevin. I'm going to wait for the dog."

"Come on, Katy. It's too risky."

"No. I'm not leaving without the dog. He's coming."

She's right. Moments later, the GPS nose brings YoYo to her side.

The group runs through what seems like miles of towering trees and tangled growth that sting their feet until an impenetrable wall of a dense thicket stops them … probably a grove of mesquite.

"Where do we go now? It's impossible to get through this. Look at those thorns."

"I soooo wish I had used my Blackberry on the bus. We would be out of here by now."

They collapse, exhausted, and worried that those scary men will catch up to them. The twins adjust their crop-top bras and groom each other like little monkeys. Sibel combs Mabel's hair with her fingers, and pulls out chunks of mud. Mabel reciprocates, running her hands over Sibel's head to smooth her dirty hair. The session ends with neat, pitch-black hair that frames matching almond eyes and cookie-cutter pug noses. They're the only ones worried about keeping up appearances.

"I want my doggie," Chrissie complains again. So where is YoYo? They look around. He was here a moment ago. Where did he go? They search the area calling, "Puppy, puppy, come," without success. From somewhere inside the thicket there is a bark. Then a series of barks. But there is no sign of YoYo.

Scotty peers through the thicket. He parts some of the thorny branches and slides under them. He crawls forward, muttering, "Ouch! Wow! Hey, some of these thorns are—ouch—three inches—ouch—long." He disappears as if swallowed up.

His sister is nervous. "Scotty, where are you? Scotty?"

"In here, sis, with the dog."

"What?"

"It's neat in here. Like a little room. Come on in."

They take turns holding back the thorny branches amidst a chorus of groans and complaints. Willie goes in first, then Tommy and Vickie. The twins require a wider opening. Entwined and inseparable, they crawl through together, whining in unison. Katy and Chrissie are next. Kevin reaches back to close the opening, so the men don't find it. I drop through the thicket to their little room. I do feel the thorns. Like a tickle but considering that we easily penetrate universes, planets, and even stars, it's a wonder that I feel anything. It must be empathy.

Inside, the space is dark but at least dry. For the moment they feel safe, and YoYo, on Chrissie's lap, gets a belly rub. In between strokes, he gets in a lick on her hand. Both of them make soft, contented sounds. Vickie still carries on about her Blackberry and how long she worked to get it, and the stuff she had to put up with from the spoiled kids she babysat.

"It's sooo weird without it."

They do get sooo used to those high-tech accoutrements.

Everyone hushes when they hear the men talking right outside the entrance to the thicket. They are looking for the children. Kevin and Katy again act like a team. They lean their heads together and whisper.

"Katy, we have to find a way out of here. Those guys are out there. I don't know what they want, but they scare me."

"Me too, Kevin. You know, I've been thinking. Thinking about the little dog. We never would have saved Chrissie without him. He found this place for us. Maybe he's our lucky charm."

"Katy, he's just a little dog, not a miracle worker."

How I would love to interject "Oh yeah?" But I must content myself with observing. With all this activity, there is no progress to report on YoYo's linguistic abilities. On the other hand, there is a lot to be said for his valiant efforts to help the children. That's why I wonder about the Committee. Does this mission have other goals? Or are YoYo and I caught up in serendipity?

"It doesn't have to be a miracle, Kevin," Katy replies. "He seems pretty smart. He found a way in here. Maybe he can find a way for us to get out of here too. Anyway, I'm beginning to really like him … a lot."

Like him? He is the most lovable, adorable, cuddly, cute little bugger I ever knew. When I have to go back, I'm going to miss him. Until, of course, the day he joins us in the Dimension.

They don't move and are silent, so the men don't discover them. It does give them a much-needed chance to rest, because they're exhausted. Tommy is on his stomach, and Scotty rests his head on Tommy's back. Vickie lies next to Tommy. The twins insist that Willie move to the other side of the room before they curl into a tight ball. Only Chrissie naps—with YoYo licking her salty tears. I want to nod too, but I hear noises. It's YoYo. The children hear it, too, and look for him. But he's gone.

"The dog's disappeared. Here we go again."

Scotty looks at all his scratches. "Hey, this time it's your turn, Tommy. I'm not going in those thorns again."

"Okay, okay. Chill out. I'll look for him." He crawls into the branches. "Oh my gawd. It's a hole. The dog's right here in a deep hole. Hey, dog. What're ya doin' in there? Com'ere."

YoYo gets yanked out, and Chrissie grabs him so he can't escape.

They examine the hole and discover it's more than a foot wide.

"It looks like a tunnel of some kind."

"Yeah. It could belong to a fox, or a coyote."

"Or a mountain lion—or even a bear."

That scares Scotty. "Hey, I'm outta here."

"Shhhhh." Vickie puts her finger to her lips. "Hear that? They discovered our hiding place. They're coming in after us."

Indeed they are coming, but it won't be easy for them. The big guys can't crawl through the way the children did. They'll have to fight their way through. And they will, which means that the tunnel, if it is a tunnel, may be the only possible escape route.

"I'll go in first and check it out," Kevin offers. "If it's okay, I'll signal, and you can follow me."

One of the most difficult things for a human to do is to go underground. Many people don't even like to go in a basement. If it's dark, damp, and perhaps dangerous, it's even more difficult. Kevin is brave to volunteer.

He steps into the hole, bends to look into the tunnel, and stands up. His face is chalk-white. His gulps and swallows indicate second thoughts. Katy says, "This may not be a good idea," but Kevin takes a deep breath, drops to his knees, and inserts his head into the hole. It's no more than a foot high, so he plops on his bare tummy and squirms forward before the others see how he trembles. Katy and Vickie clasp hands to reassure each other. Chrissie squats down and looks into the hole.

"Why did Kevin go in that hole?" she asks.

The twins answer, "He wants to save us from the men outside."

Chrissie doesn't understand, and it's just as well.

Loud thrashing and curses announce the progress the men make, slashing their way through the mesquite.

"Oh, please, Kevin, find us a way out before the men get in," Vickie whispers. "I'm soooo scared." YoYo squirms out of Chrissie's arms and jumps into the hole. No way is he going to be left behind if there's action somewhere. Chrissie cries, "Puppy, puppy, come back," and drops into the hole to go after him. The others pull her out.

"He'll come back. Kevin will bring him back," they reassure her in spite of their own fears, urging her to be quiet so the men don't hear them.

Minutes seem like an eternity to them. Not to me, of course. I have all the time in the world, so I can be patient, but I do want to see what YoYo is up to. He was chattering funny *Urh ... urh ... urh* sounds when he jumped in. Through his nose. Maybe it was cyber-powered sniffing. Underground is new territory for him.

YoYo runs with ease in the darkness for about thirty feet to catch up to Kevin struggling on his muddy belly, every inch a challenge. YoYo slips in front of Kevin, his nose working. Now he's a guide dog. There must be a problem because the sniffs turn noisy. YoYo is doing the bark-rant signal. It echoes throughout the tunnel. Here's the problem. He's warning Kevin that they've reached a sharp drop in the tunnel. YoYo leads the way, and Kevin rides the mud down to the bottom. The tunnel is wider and deeper at this lower depth, so Kevin can crawl through the muck on hands and knees. Water drips on him.

"You know, little dog," he whispers to the critter sidled next to him, "I think we're going to find a way out. I think we're going to make it. Katy was right. You are going to save us."

In response, Kevin gets a lick on his mud-caked hand. YoYo doesn't seem at all rattled by the tunnel. In fact, he's a bit excited. Maybe it's a new game—a kind of hide-and-seek?

"It's okay, the tunnel's okay," Kevin shouts.

The kids hear Kevin's muffled shouts. It's the signal they hoped for. Now it's their turn to descend into the dark hole—their only choice because the slashing sounds punctuated by curses are getting louder.

The boys are obliged to show bravado. Willie snuggles in, followed by Tommy and Scotty, who complains, "Hey, how am I supposed to move in all this mud?"

Willie suggests, "You can go back."

Scotty, plopping on his belly, wisecracks back, "Yeah, you're so funny, Willie. I'm going to die laughing in here." As usual, there is a problem with the twins. They can't fit in together. Separating is difficult if not impossible. They discuss it in a nonverbal exchange—looks, nods, and head shakes, and Mabel jumps into the hole. And jumps out.

"I'm afraid. I won't go in there." She's crying. No bravado here.

The thrashing gets closer.

"I'll go." Vickie crawls into the tunnel and disappears.

"Chrissie, it's your turn. Go find your puppy."

Chrissie enthusiastically crawls into the earth. To her, it's just another adventure. The twins still hang back.

"Girls," Katy tells them, "if you're not going, I am. You can wait for the men. Hear that? It won't be long." Sibel drops her sister's hand, moves in front of Katy, and crawls in. Mabel, now bawling, hangs back. "Bye." Katy disappears. Mabel is alone. But not for long. Moments later, Katy feels someone behind her. I'll go on record that this is the first time the twins have been separated since birth. Now they are all in the tunnel. Where will it take them? I float above ground to watch their progress.

Oh no! No! No! Something terrible just happened. There was a big roar, and the entrance to the tunnel caved in. The hole they crawled into is gone! It's filled with wet mud. Thank heaven it didn't cave in on the children. But now they can't go back. They must move forward and quickly. The whole tunnel is unstable. Water drips from the roof, and if it caves in, they'll be crushed. No one will ever find them. Please, Committee, tell me what to do to get them out of there!

The only sound is the wind rustling through the trees.

Chapter Sixteen

I feel helpless and frustrated. Terrified. Even if I could warn the children, would it make any difference? They're trapped. The only thing I can do is monitor the situation from above. See what's happening underground—an invaluable accommodation from the Committee in this situation. It's been an eye-opener for me. I've learned how space can be manipulated. How it can be used. Human knowledge is sketchy at best. Scientists recently discovered that space is like a web. Well, yes, it is, and it's flexible too. Now I think of space as a giant trampoline that I use. I become a projectile traveling at the speed of light, and that's how I can be in several places at the same time. It's like having the ability to watch two screens—one is LA, the other, DC. Thank the Celestials for that. Unfortunately, though, it doesn't help me save the children. Hold on. Here comes a new vision. It's the driver of the semi—the one that blocked the Toyota on the mountain road. He's talking to the cops. I zoom in tighter—I want to hear this.

"I was suspicious when the school bus passed me. That was crazy. The bus almost tipped over. School buses aren't supposed to do that, so I knew something was wrong. By the time that car could get around me, the bus disappeared, probably onto one of the side roads. Yeah, two men were in the car."

That's good information, and squads rush out to check those roads. The first one dead-ends in the forest—no signs of the bus. The next two cars drive all the way to the river's edge, but there are no signs of the bus or footprints in the mud. Another squad checks out the fourth road—the one the bus took—and hits the same mud. Its wheels spin, sink, and stop. Someone moves in the woods nearby. The cops jump out in pursuit, but they slip and slide in the mud while their shoes fill with water, slowing them down. The figure disappears into the woods. The cops struggle on until they reach the shore where the kids had their temporary camp. The remains of a fire are still warm. Kids' clothing and shoes are draped on the rocks with a waterlogged cell phone. Nearby, the Toyota is still sinking into the mud. The registration shows that the owner is a known Sinaloa gang member.

Captain MacDonald reacts to their report.

"So drugs are involved. That means we need to deploy more resources. The park's a huge area to cover. We could do it if we had the time. But we don't. Can't waste a minute, or those kids might not make it. Got to call the governor for help. The National Guard has search-and-rescue teams trained for this job."

The governor understands the urgency and breaks precedent to order a National Guard unit to assist. Nine kids' lives are at stake, and bureaucratic rules are broken. A control center is set up at the river. FBI agents join the search teams because the park is federal land. Their regional director, Hal Brocklehurst, checks in with the captain.

"There's a rumor, Captain, and I do hope it's a rumor, that a little dog was on the bus."

Hey, I know that guy. He's the same fellow who was at the federal building during the terrorist episode.

"Yes," the captain responds, "as implausible as it sounds, it could be our little Demon Dog. He was reported lost on the same street."

"That could be bad news—or good news, if he's with the children."

The captain glares at him.

"You have to agree that YoYo has a record of effectiveness against criminals."

"I prefer to use our methods, especially when children are involved. How do you know it won't bite the kids? My grandchild was on that bus, and I know she would be scared to death of that dog. I hope we can rescue them before it does any harm. That dog should wear a muzzle. They didn't call him Demon Dog for nothing."

How I'm going to enjoy it when you eat those words. And here's a word of advice, Captain. If you still want to be district attorney, drop the "Muzzle the dog" line.

New vision. It's Hector. Almost forgot about him. Got to keep track of his whereabouts. This amazing gift that allows me to be in more than one place at the same time is called omnipresence, for which I thank the Celestials. I'm not sure I even knew what omnipresent meant. But I sure do now and have a word of advice for humans: These perks are terrific. So don't screw up.

Hector is watching the police activity from a ridge. Oops. A helicopter zooms overhead, and he dives under a silver fir, using its wide, silver-blue branches for cover. Hector's beginning to understand how big his problems are, and he's scared. Real scared.

It isn't just the drugs. It's the kids. They'll accuse me of kidnapping them. I didn't even know they were on the bus. So how could I have kidnapped them? But why did José and Adolpho stop chasing me and go after the kids? O mi Dios! They want the kids for ... ransom. If anything happens to them, they'll blame me. I'll be held responsible.

He collapses on a rock only to scream "Oooooowwww" and quickly jumps up. He forgot about the painful burns on his backside.

What should I do? Turn myself in? It's my bad luck. And it's bad luck for those poor kids too.

Isn't it a little late to worry about the kids, Hector? What nerve. How callous ... now that's strange. He looks into my space as if he heard me and answers, "Better late than never." Sometimes I wonder what my abilities to communicate with humans are—that is, besides occasionally touching an aura with a wing. I was told that I couldn't communicate with humans. Could they have meant that I *shouldn't* communicate with them?

Hector decides to surrender and heads down the mountain. He stops at the crest of a ridge to get the cops' attention. But the cops are at the other end of the woods, totally preoccupied, and have no idea he wants to surrender. He sees the empty squad car that got stuck. Now there is a second car next to it. Thoughts rumble through Hector's head.

That must be an unmarked squad. Maybe undercover. I wonder ... could

I? No, it's too crazy to even think about. Both cars are empty. What if ... what if ... I could get to it and hide in the backseat of the unmarked car? Cops always ride in the front seat. Maybe I'll get caught. But maybe I won't. If I stay here, for sure they'll catch me. I'll take the risk.

He whimpers in pain with each movement and limps to the car. It's unlocked. He crawls in. His short stature pays off. He fits perfectly on the floor. If his luck has changed for the better, the cops won't look in the backseat.

Nudging the space trampoline, I close the screen on Hector as he settles in the car and descend into the tunnel with the kids. They're inching forward on their stomachs, sliding downhill, deeper into the pitch-black mountain. It's not fast enough, but at least they're not trembling now. Mabel's sobbing has stopped, and there hasn't been another cave-in. Yet. But that Willie is up to something. What's with him? Of all things, in this situation, he's telling a ghost story, and they don't like it.

"No!" they scream, already scared enough.

"Okay, okay. So you don't like ghost stories. Anyone know any jokes?"

Jokes? I don't believe he said that. I wouldn't want to be telling jokes, or hearing jokes, when I'm in a deep, dark hole, not sure I'm going to get out. There is, however, a reason behind Willie's joke idea. He remembers the time he and his family drove to Nebraska to visit relatives and encountered a tornado. It touched ground, picked up cars and hurled them in the air, and uprooted giant trees. His dad pulled off the road into a ditch just in time, so it missed them. His sister was hysterical with fear. Vickie couldn't stop crying no matter how many times her mom and dad told her the tornado was gone. Dad tried a different tactic.

"Honey, do you remember that old car that Grandma used to drive?"

Through sniffles there was a tentative "Yes."

"Well, that car had seen better days. It was mostly hung together with duct tape. Remember?"

"Yeah, and it had a big dent in the side."

"Right. More than one. Backing out of the garage was a problem for her. One day she called me at work, upset.

"'That danged old car!' she snorted. 'The brakes went out. Can you come and get me?'

"I said, 'Okay. Where are you?'

"'At the drugstore,' she told me.

"'And where's the car?' I asked.

"'It's right here. In the drugstore with me.'"

Vickie laughed at the punch line. Before she could go back to sobbing, he had another one.

"Grandma was a character, wasn't she? Remember when she went to the doctor and told him that every time she took a sip of tea, she had a sharp pain in her eye?"

Vickie and Willie were paying attention. They knew their dad was up to something.

"He told her to try taking the spoon out of the cup."

"Daaad!" But the crying stopped. Willie had picked up the routine.

"What do you get when you put a car and a pet together?"

She knew that one. "A carpet." She had one of her own.

"Dad, I know how you can double your money. Fold it in half." With that, a smile came through, and the crisis was over. When the sun came out, Dad and Willie pushed the car out of the ditch, while Vickie steered under Mom's direction. They sang the rest of the way. That experience taught Willie a valuable lesson that he's putting to good use right now. The kids aren't crying, but they are scared. Let's see if his therapy works.

Katy breaks the silence with, "Why is the river so rich?"

There's no response until ... "Because it has two banks." That's Kevin.

A catcall, and, "Smarty-pants."

It's good medicine and takes their mind off the danger. And I'm glad they can't see all the spiders, disturbed by the invaders and running back to their nests, or the hundreds, maybe thousands, of worms wiggling to safety deeper in the ground.

"What did the banana say to the elephant who stepped on it?" Tommy asks, but no one has an answer. "Nothing. Bananas can't talk." That brings some giggles.

Vickie offers a story. "Sooo. A police officer sees a lady with a penguin.

He tells her, 'Lady, take the penguin to the zoo.' Sooo, the next day, he sees the same lady with the penguin.

"'Lady, I thought I told you to take the penguin to the zoo.' The lady replies, 'Oh yes, I did. And he loved it. Today I'm taking him to Disneyland.'"

They laugh a lot at that one. Except for Scotty. He has a delayed reaction. Willie can't resist. "Wise man say, he who laughs last, didn't get joke."

Tommy defends his brother. "Willie, if you had a brain, it'd be lonely."

Scotty recovers. "Hey! What has four legs and can't walk?"

They all scream, "A table!"

That joke has been around forever; even the Committee has heard it.

Willie again. "That's sthuuupid!"

Vickie tells her brother to apologize to Scotty.

"Okay. I'm sorry you're sthuuupid!"

The twins offer, in unison: "There was a man who had his left side cut off. But he's all right now." They laugh hilariously at their own joke.

Trying to outdo each other with jokes and laughing so hard, they sometimes forget to crawl. I'd like to prod their—uh—auras. But then we hear, "I see light … look, there's a light." The light is close. That means they are near the end of the tunnel. They can get out. Thank you.

Horrors! Disaster! The roof of the tunnel just caved in. The light disappeared. I spoke too soon. Now tons of wet mud block their exit. It's the disaster I feared.

"Dear Committee," I beg. "Please help me. I thought the children were saved, but now they are entombed in this tunnel. Oxygen will give out. They'll be asphyxiated."

Do I hear an answer? No. Only silence. I try again.

"Remember the Mission? YoYo is in there too, you know." Still no answer. I must do something. Even if it means breaking the rules. If only I knew which rules to break.

The children are silent. Kevin is the first to speak. "Is everyone okay?"

Weak answers drift to him with cries of despair.

"What happened?"

That's what I'd like to know.

"So, where's the light?" and a hysterical "We're going to die."

Shaking, Kevin feels his way in the dark until he hits a wall of mud.

"We have to dig our way out."

Tommy worms his way next to him.

"Maybe we should try to go back?"

Someone agrees. "Yeah, let's back up and get out of here."

"But those men are looking for us."

Kevin remembers something his father preached: Use logic. "Let's think about it. How about this? What if we try to dig through this, and if we can't, we go back."

Are they capable of making an important decision like this? They're in shock and terrified.

Willie responds, "I say, let's go for it. Start digging. I'm right behind you."

Scotty wakes from his paralysis. "Hey, me too."

The girls huddle together in a small space. YoYo is tucked under Chrissie's arm, panting hard. He has picked up the pheromones of fear that ooze from the kids. He's frustrated that none of his protective techniques will work down here. As for the mission, there's not much chance of a word in here. Unless it's "out," which would be more than appropriate.

In a firm voice, Katy tells Mabel, "You have to stop saying we're going to die. We're not. They're digging through the mud. Hear them? They'll find a way through."

Vickie is not as diplomatic. "Yeah, Mabel. So shut up. I don't want to hear that anymore."

Scotty reports, "Hey, I felt Tommy's feet move."

They can't see a thing in the black tunnel, but he did feel Tommy's feet go forward several inches.

"They got through."

The boys have scratched, poked, and clawed at the mud and made a space for Kevin to wiggle into. Tommy, Scotty, and Willie follow him. My goodness. If only their parents could see them now, see how they fight for their lives, how proud they would be. I want to help them, but all I can do is embrace their auras, stroke them like violins, creating chords that give them confidence and courage. There can't be a rule against that. Besides, what are they gonna do? Spank me? I don't think so. There's no punishment in the Dimension.

Good lord! It's happening again. The whole tunnel shakes violently with a deafening roar that drowns out the children's screams. Mud tumbles in, filling the space behind them. Katy cries out, "Kevin, the tunnel filled with mud. We can't go back. Hurry! Please hurry! Get us out of here!"

The girls quickly escape into the narrow wet space the boys carved out. Vickie slides in first, the twins crawl behind her, and Katy drags Chrissie with her, barely escaping another avalanche of mud. But YoYo doesn't make it. Chrissie drops him, and he is buried in the mud that pours down. This is terrible. He's trying to scratch his way out. Four paws dig, fighting to survive, but the mud keeps piling up on him. He attempts to bark but instead chokes. If the children don't remember him and come back for him, this will be YoYo's end. I know it's unreasonable to expect them to turn around and go back for a dog. But it's my YoYo. If only I could use my reward to make a wish and save him.

I can't help but ask how these children could forget about the dog who saved them. It isn't right. Then I tell myself, "Angela, look at the positive side. The children are okay. They'll get out." Yeah, but I'm hurting right along with YoYo. It's unbearably painful to lie beside him and not be able to help. Of course I won't leave him. I'll wait for the end.

Well, the children are not okay. Once again, I was overly optimistic and spoke too soon. They are coughing and choking. They can't breathe. The oxygen level is so low that I fear asphyxiation. There has to be a way to get some air in here. I can't lose YoYo and the children.

"Committee, I implore you, please help—before it's too late. If this is a test of some kind, I object. It's unfair."

Off the record, I'd love to tell the Committee, "Hey, guys, get with the program." Do I need to remind them that losing YoYo is unthinkable? That he is the one dog in the world they selected to pioneer a first in nature—to determine whether two species can communicate with one language? Their pet project. I was brought up to respect my elders, and "elders" puts it mildly, but this simply cannot be the way the mission ends. It means I'll never hear that *HehHehHeh* again.

"There's light." Kevin pokes at a pinhole and light floods into the area they've been scratching through.

Only one more pile of mud blocks them. They frantically dig through it and step into a large, bright cave. It's dotted with pools, carved out from years of dripping water. Shivering, the girls follow and move toward the warm sunlight, looking like blackened statues. The boys try rinsing their feet in the frigid water. Scotty works on his toes.

"Hey, toejam was never this bad," he says, scooping out the mud caked between his toes. The girls scrape the gobs that pad their knees and hands. Only Chrissie remembers YoYo. She rushes back to the hole calling, "Doggie, here Doggie. Doggie."

"The dog's still in the tunnel."

"He must be buried. Oh no!"

"I thought he was with Chrissie the whole time."

"He was. I thought he was behind us," Katy offers.

"We have to find him." That's Willie, the dog-lover.

"No. We shouldn't go back in there. We're lucky we got out."

"That's not fair, after all he did for us. I'm going back."

"Willie, you can't do it."

With a defiant "Who says?" Willie disappears into the tunnel.

He's my best hope for YoYo. I don't know whether he'll succeed, but he'll try hard.

Crawling inside the dark tunnel, Willie glides his hands along the floor, searching for YoYo, running his fingers through every pile of mud. If only YoYo could signal his presence, but he can't make a sound. In fact, YoYo's not moving. His body is stiff and cold.

Willie hits a solid wall that stops him. Crying, he pounds at it with fists. Defeated, he turns to go back.

That little dog is in there. If I leave, he will die.

Right, Willie. He will die. You are my only hope. We've been abandoned.

Raw fingertips again tear into the mud. It's gotten as hard as concrete.

"I'm not giving up, little dog. I'm comin'."

"What's this?" he mutters, feeling something soft. He gropes for the muddy object.

"I've got him," Willie shouts.

"I've got you, little fella. Don't you worry," Willie reassures YoYo, tugging the ravaged body out of the mud. YoYo's head lolls back. He doesn't move. Willie's valiant rescue may be in vain. Still, I can't believe it's YoYo's time to go. He has important work to do. This mission has been full of twists and turns, surprises and shocks, but will it end with this cold, limp, motionless body? Where is my vibrant, exuberant puppy? Will I never hear the bark-rant and the happy greeting and see the speeding pendulum?

Willie tucks YoYo securely under his arm as water pours into the tunnel. Like an eel, he glides through it until he reaches the cave where the children wait to help him out. The limp body in Willie's arms shocks them.

Scotty declares, "Hey. It's dead."

Katy takes YoYo from Willie, and rocks him in her arms. "Wake up, little dog. Wake up. You're safe now," she whispers to him.

Chrissie cries, pulling at the body. "I want my doggie."

YoYo's legs droop from Katy's arms.

Willie despairs. "I tried. I tried to save him."

"We know you did. You tried your best. He was a good dog."

"He was such a good dog."

"Let's put him down now," Kevin says. "I don't think we can help him anymore."

Katy kneels and gently places YoYo's body on the stone floor, his stiff legs outstretched.

The weeping twins pat his head. "Bye-bye, little dog."

"Little dog. That's what we kept calling him. Why didn't we give him a name? Huh?" Willie asks. "He should have a name. Think how lucky we were that he was with us."

"You're right, Willie. You know what? We should give him a name. We should call him Lucky."

"Yeah, Katy. That's a good dog name."

Heads shake in agreement.

"So Lucky it is." Willie dips his hand into a pool of cold water, sprinkles it onto YoYo's head, and intones in a deep, baritone voice, "Cute little dog, we ... uh ... loved you. We ... uh ... appreciate you. We're so sorry to see you go. But we're not going to let you leave without a proper name, so I hereby dub you—Lucky."

It may sound strange—I don't mean to veer from the action—but do you hear Willie's voice? I'm reminded of something. It may be irrelevant, but the baritone voice that Willie fakes now for his "I hereby dub you" will become his permanently at age thirteen. That's when his larynx drops lower, a phenomenon previously explained. I apologize if the interruption annoyed anyone up there.

The children stare in disbelief at the collapsed ears that once stood at attention, the fluffy coat now sculpted in mud on a tiny body with a mere cigar stub of a tail.

"We'll miss you, Lucky," Vickie murmurs, kneeling to pet him one last time. Chrissie doesn't understand and lifts YoYo's head into her lap. She lowers her face and looks into his eyes.

"He can't see me. Is that why he's dead?"

Nobody answers. Except for the constant drip of water, there is silence.

"Maybe we should say a prayer."

"I know one," Sibel offers. "Now Lucky lays down to sleep, I pray the Lord his soul to keep. Oh ... I forgot ... Mabel, do you remember what comes after that?"

"It's ... it's ... If he should die before he wakes, I pray the Lord his soul to take."

Heads bow with a collective "Amen."

A tearful Scotty turns away from the scene. He wants to escape and walks to the cave's opening. "Hey, there's a river right beneath us."

Nobody pays any attention, and he wanders out alone to explore. Minutes later he rushes back in, startling the kids and interrupting their reverie.

"Hey, you are not going to believe what's out there."

Eight faces register terror. I want to warn him, "Please, no more shocks. I don't think they can take any more."

"Hey, take it easy, guys. I found a berry field. Look at this." He hands Kevin a fat, deep-red berry.

"It's a boysenberry. No, it's our lunch. Let's go."

Thank heaven children are resilient. They can recover from shock and grief quickly.

One more good-bye to YoYo, and the very muddy kids step out of the cave, stopping to look back at the tragic figure lying so still. Now my precious YoYo is alone—except for me. And what can I do? Can I wave a wand full of energy that will revive him, make his body warm, and bring him back? Something, anything, because I don't want to leave him. Tears flow. My tears. Yes, angels can weep.

A voice says, *The children.*

My orders. I must leave YoYo to his fate. Reluctantly, I obey and join the children outside.

Scotty did find a big patch of berries in the middle of the forest. It seems like a miracle, but more likely a bird accidentally dropped a seed that germinated in the rich, damp soil. One healthy bush spread and grew into the large, rambling patch the children raid. They stuff themselves with delicious, juicy berries, paying no attention to the thorns that stuck them. Katy, the worrier, warns, "You know, it could be hours before they find us. Let's save some for later."

"Where we gonna keep them?"

Willie again has a solution. "We'll make baskets. I learned at summer camp!"

Summer camp really paid off.

He shows them how to weave twigs into little containers that are soon filled with berries.

"What's that?" A weird sound comes from the cave. Well, well, well. The sound is coming from a small, muddy figure. It strains to bark and then collapses. YoYo. So either I was tricked into believing he had died, or the Committee stepped in and did the Celestial thing. You know, "walking on water" and "the fishes and the loaves." YoYo rises like a phoenix from the ashes except he staggers out and falls in a clump. Thin, weak *rrruurrr … rrruurrrs* rasp out as breathy *rrruurr … rrruuurrrs*. With a huge effort, he raises his head to look at them. But his eyes shift to something else … something above them. Whatever it is, it provokes another attempt to bark. He wobbles to a rock and tries to jump on it but falls back—his rear legs give in. I know one thing for sure: he may not be in any shape for an attack, but however lame those *rrruurrrs* may be, they do have a message.

Willie is the first to recover from the shock. "It's the dog. He's not dead."

"No. He was soooo dead. It's gotta be a ghost."

"It's Lucky, and he's no ghost. Let's get him."

"Yeah, but something's upsetting him." Kevin follows YoYo's line of vision.

"Oh my gawd. It's a bear!"

He's right. It is a large black bear headed for the berry patch. YoYo's nose quivers at a brand-new scent.

Now the question is, should I warn him to back off? Bears are uncharted territory for a terrier of any size. Or tell him to take it easy on the bear. I'd say the odds are with YoYo. But then I always liked long shots … ignored the favorites at 2/1 and put my money on the 28/1 ponies.

"Run," shouts Willie.

"Run back to the cave," Kevin commands. "Run, run, run."

That's it! That's what YoYo's been trying to tell you! Just switch an *r* to the difficult *n*, and *rrruurrr … rrrruurrr* becomes *rrrruunnn … rrruuunnn*.

Kevin picks up some rocks on the way back to the cave—something to throw at the bear.

"The cave could belong to the bear."

Right, but it's your only refuge, so you'd better get in there fast, kiddos. With humans, there are some possibilities, but with bears, I have no influence.

The six-hundred-pound black bear lumbers up the rocks to the berry patch. It wanders through it with ease. Thick, scruffy fur provides protection from the thorns. It stands on hind legs with long snout extended to nibble at the berries. After a leisurely feast, we hear a grunt, which could be a bear version of a belch, an "I've had enough" signal, and the bear ambles toward the cave. Small black eyes watch the bear with interest. YoYo can't even stand up, so how does he think he can mount a defense against a bear? I can't go through this again. I smack his head multiple times with energized zaps to give him the message: YoYo, this is suicidal. He shakes them off and begins a series of sharp, staccato *woouuff ... wwoouuff ... wwoouuffs*.

So he intends to begin his defense with the wolf's superbark. The next step is to assume the straight and tense posture of the wolf. The hair on his shoulders should be upright and stiff, ears straight up. His glands should spill out a defense odor that announces: All systems are ready to engage. Alas, they are not. None of this is happening. In fact, the wolf bark collapses into a wheezy cough. So much for his defense strategy. Now must I witness the little warrior's final battle? Did I say "battle"? There's no battle in the crumpled creature, whose ears are back, way back. Yes, YoYo is scared. Me too.

Come on, YoYo, I whisper, whizzing around and into his ears. Let's give it one more try. I'll be your cheering section. I'll zap the bear as he approaches, to slow him down a little.

YoYo doesn't move. The bear keeps approaching, totally ignoring my efforts to slow him with zaps in his ear, his eyes, and other sensitive areas. He stands over YoYo, looking down at him. I know all is lost when a giant paw languidly reaches out to grab him. But YoYo surprises us. Somehow he finds the strength to roll over, away from the bear, into a sitting position. This is your chance, YoYo, I want to shout. Scoot—fast—into the cave. Oh my. What is it he's doing? Sitting still just staring into the bear's eyes? This is foolhardy. It won't work. YoYo, you can't stare a bear down.

Hmmm. It appears that's not his strategy. He has another plan. With a few quick limping steps over to the bear, he snaps at its leg. That took a lot of courage. Those little teeth probably didn't penetrate that big, hairy leg, but it was a surprise attack. The bear rears up on his hind legs. But a six-foot bear is not tall enough to scare YoYo. He reconnoiters to bite the bear again.

The children watch from the safety of the cave and scream, "No, Lucky, no."

Chrissie cries, "Please, Lucky, come here. Please, Lucky, come."

The bear blinks in confusion. Maybe it did feel something. It roars in anger. *Grrrrr-rrrrr!* A voice so deep, I feel the vibration.

YoYo answers, but he has to lean back on his haunches to force out an irritating *rrrooouuufff*. Well, I know that's what he meant to do, but what came out was a sneezed *roo-cho* along with a wad of mud stuffed in his nostrils. He'd be embarrassed, but plugged ears prevent him from hearing himself. He'll go down fighting because he has a job to do. My YoYo's back!

Eye-to-eye, they glare at each other until the bear lunges. Bears are fast, and their claws lethal. And big. YoYo is small but agile He dodges the claws and crawls around the bear, nips the foot and stops, waiting for the bear to react. It does. The feet are more vulnerable than the leg. If the bite didn't hurt, at least it pinched him. The big head points down, and a deep snarl thunders from his throat. *Aarrrooogggghhh.* I hear a lot of frustration in it too. This little creature is probably unlike anything it has ever encountered. The bear pauses with a limp, outstretched paw, considering the next move. He chooses an infamous bear strategy: Pretend disinterest until the prey lets its defenses down. The bear looks away, paying no attention to YoYo. But YoYo is not fooled by bear strategy, and he keeps a wary eye on it. Now that his sinuses are clear, he emits an *Mmmaaammm*. A lot of *m*'s. Not exactly a bark. Then there's a second syllable—*uufff*.

I repeat the two totally different sounds several times. Two separate words? In this desperate situation, could it be another breakthrough? Maybe an actual sentence? This demands immediate analysis.

Mmmaaaamm is coming from his nose, the *uufff* from his throat. Both systems used. I haven't heard either of these sounds before. I play with the words phonetically, trying to understand the meaning. We know consonants are a problem, so I revert to my routine of running through the alphabet to replace them, one at a time. Nothing interesting comes up. Wait! *N* is a possibility. I spell it out. *Mmmmaaannn.*

Now to work on the *ufffff.* Again, I replace the *f*'s with all the consonants. *B, C, D, E, F, G, H, I, J, K, L, M, N, O, P* … Aha! Nothing makes sense until I get to the *P.* Can *uuff* be "up"? Of course it is. YoYo's telling the bear to "Man up." He is a little devil.

Please note that he didn't learn this from me. But he heard it somewhere. That means that dogs do pick up the words they hear. They fool us into thinking they're lying there, just licking their paws, while they're actually listening to every word. Now we know that humans should watch their language around children and dogs. It wouldn't matter except that now language is a possibility for dogs. Someday, people might have to wash their dogs' mouths out with soap. Maybe right now "possibility" is too strong, but long-term it's a probability, from what the Committee has indicated. Either way, even if I could tell the folks, would they believe me? No, they have to wait a little longer for that surprise.

The insulted bear pounces, and giant claws grab YoYo. He wrestles to escape, biting a long black snout. Ouch. I know that one hurt—all noses are sensitive. The bear drops YoYo, but can he move fast enough to escape? No, he can't. Back legs collapse, and the bear snatches him up, disappearing in the woods, YoYo gripped in giant jaws. The children scream. Chrissie and the twins sob, while the boys rub their eyes. Yes, YoYo found a way into their hearts. He has a habit of doing that.

"The bear will eat him."

We know who responds with: "No, it won't. I'll bet you anything Lucky gets away and comes back—alive."

Katy bets. So I'm not the only one. But nobody keeps track down here, because vices don't count for much. The Dimension has a higher standard. Fortunately for me, there's some tolerance. That's how I got a second chance. Heaven only knows; I may need a third.

"Well, Lucky better come back soon. This must be the bear's cave. We can't stay here."

A helicopter flies overhead, but the pilot doesn't spot the children, and their hopes are dashed.

"They didn't see us."

"What I wouldn't give for my cell phone."

"They know we're in here somewhere," Kevin consoles them. "Let's move higher so they can see us if they come back."

It's a slow climb because their bare feet struggle on the sharp rocks. Chrissie rides on Tommy's back until he tires, and Kevin takes over.

"I hear barking." Vickie stops to listen. "It's Lucky."

They call his new name over and over, but no Lucky appears. They continue to climb, and now it's the twins turn: "We hear Lucky. We hear him."

Again, they're disappointed because Lucky doesn't show up. The path turns downward into a forest filled with sounds of animals scurrying. Rabbits stand frozen at the intrusion before they hop away. Overhead, squirrels leap from tree to tree. Scotty stumbles on a stack of brittle, dead sticks. It looks like a little house. Something runs out of it. It's ... it's a rat. Not an ordinary rat, however. It's a little brown Mohave wood rat with dainty feet that it uses to climb trees. But it is a rat, and it spooks the girls.

The forest turns dark with trees so tall and dense that light can't penetrate. Unless I miss my guess, they're probably white fir closed canopy pines. Owls wake from their nests and call to each other. Even the boys are spooked now, but they stay on the path. Something hits Katy's shoulder. She looks up to see a chipmunk that scolds and throws another acorn at her. Everyone is scared, but Willie has a different take on it.

"I think we're in a fairy tale. This is the woods that Hansel and Gretel were in."

In the background there is a low roar. It's not a bear roar, and it gets louder. Katy jokes, "And I suppose that's Hansel and Gretel calling."

"It's water," Tommy yells. "It's a giant waterfall. We discovered a waterfall." They have, indeed, and it's an amazing sight. Torrents of water cascade down the mountainside, dropping into a deep-blue pool that overflows, spilling into the river below. Thundering water drowns out a lot of the "Amazing," "Awesome," and "Wow" remarks that the kids utter as they marvel at the scene, water splashing them.

"Hey, this is like taking a shower," Scotty declares, moving into the spray.

Lush grasses and golden poppies cover the ground like a thick, colorful carpet.

A dark shadow, a blanket of orange, drifts past them. It hovers and moves to a nearby tree, wrapping itself around the trunk.

"Butterflies," they shout.

The boys run to it. The girls watch open-mouthed as hundreds, maybe thousands, of butterflies settle on the tree's branches. A few glide down to the pool for a drink. Scotty reaches up to grab one. Katy stops him just in time.

"Don't touch them. They're monarch butterflies. They're in danger of extinction. They're a protected species. You can get in big trouble."

"Hey, I just wanted to get a good look at those black-and-white polka dots."

A second group flutters over their heads and lands on the golden poppies to feast on the nectar.

"They're eating. They need energy for their trip. I read about their migration from Canada." Tommy, like Kevin, is something of a bookworm.

"You mean these butterflies flew all the way from Canada?"

"Yup! And they go all the way to Mexico."

"That's soooo far. How do they know the way?"

"You know what's amazing, Vickie? They can even go back to the same tree. I can't believe I'm seeing this. I never dreamed I'd ever ... Do you know how lucky we are?"

Kevin agrees. "Yeah, and if it wasn't for the men chasing us, the bear wanting to eat us, and losing Lucky, I'd say this is a fabulous experience."

Katy is philosophical. "I hope that's the way we end up remembering it."

Scotty points at the rocks. "Hey, speaking of Lucky ... there he is."

YoYo did manage to escape the bear. He ran to a cliff and scrambled down to a narrow ledge and hid there. After a while, the bear got tired of looking for him and he left.

Chrissie runs to him. "Lucky, Lucky!"

YoYo slides down the ledge and manages a little hop over the pool, but then his legs give out, and he slumps on the ground. No wonder. His battered, mud-caked body is riddled with bloody slashes. Nevertheless, when Chrissie picks him up, a tail wiggles, and nasal sounds puff out: *ffuuufff … ffuuuufff … ffuuufff.* Her sounds are equally soft and cooing. The kids take turns hugging and petting him. He's their dog now. Their lucky dog. Hmmm? Wait a minute. Did I miss something? I'm thinking that *Ffuuufff* sounds like "luf." Maybe Barbara Walters's dog did say "I love you," the way she reported.

"So how on earth did he ever get up into that waterfall?" wonders Vickie.

"Maybe he found a way in behind it."

"Could it be another cave?"

"How many does this place have?"

The four-year-old speaks up. "No cave. No cave." They agree. So do I. No more caves.

Lucky is back with them, and the discovery of the waterfall is exciting. For a few moments, they can forget that they're stranded, lost in the wilderness of a national forest, hungry, cold, wet, and tired. And two dangerous men are chasing them while a bear lurks in the nearby woods, ready to pounce.

The question is: What will YoYo do now that he's back? More important, what will he say? Whatever it is, I'm ready to record it. Come on, YoYo. Give me a word. Even if it's all vowels, I'd be thrilled to hear it … What's that? It's impossible? A word with all vowels is impossible? No such words? How about "eeeuuuu"?

Chapter Seventeen

Katy does lookout duty to watch for their enemies—both two-legged and four-legged. The monarchs still rest in the trees. A pair of dragonflies buzz the boys while they dangle their feet in the pool. It's peaceful in the warmth of the late-afternoon sun. But Willie can't resist temptation and pushes Tommy into the pool. He laughs when Tommy pops up, spitting water. Scotty retaliates and shoves Willie in. As Willie tumbles in, he grabs Scotty, and both go under. Now the three boys wrestle, splash each other, and kick to stay afloat. YoYo sees it as violent activity and objects with *aaarrrfff … aaarrrrrfffs*. Literal translation: no roughhousing! The boys respond with splashes that send him running back to Chrissie's lap.

I've grown fond of these kids. Going to miss them when the mission ends. I can't help but wonder how they'll turn out. If this adventure will have a positive or negative effect on them. Of course, everything is known in the Dimension, and the information is kept behind a big door. But inquiries about the future are discouraged to prevent any interference. I am tempted … tempted to try for a quick peek. The door is unlocked, and no one would suspect that I would leave YoYo for the moment or two it would take. Well, I am not only a risk-taker, I'm an incurable snoop, so here goes.

Oh my. Oh my. It's not at all what I expected. So many surprises. How this adventure affects everything. I'll start with Willie. Well, I was right. He won't finish college. He'll be too impatient. This adventure plays a huge part in his future, because when the kids are rescued, the media will love them. We know what that means. Lots of publicity.

Lots of exposure for all of them. Willie will get his chance to shine on interviews, many on national TV. And he will shine. He'll do a routine that turns every challenge they faced into rip-roaring comedy … tales about YoYo beating up Hector and his escape from the bear … their barefooted escape through the woods. Even the dangerous tunnel escapade is plumbed for funny stories, not to mention YoYo's reincarnation. Yes, Willie will make people laugh, and they'll love him because we always love people who have that gift. Guest appearances will follow, and, as incredible as it sounds, Willie will have his own show, *Willie's Wit*. It will be in that famous timeslot: Saturday at 11:30 p.m. And dogs. Of course he will have lots of dogs. Rescue dogs. How appropriate, under the circumstances.

It was only a quick glance, but I saw the twins … hold on … first let's see what's happening here.

The girls laze around the waterfall while the boys play in the water. Out of the blue, Sibel and Mabel chirp, "We know a song."

Vickie encourages them. "Soooo, let's hear your song."

We're about to be treated to an impromptu concert. Sibel and Mabel take center stage on a flat rock. Water flows down the mountain behind them. Their dark, bobbed hair is in disarray, their faces smudged with dirt, and their floral bras and bikinis are still wet and grimy, but none of this stops their determination to perform. And with so much energy and enthusiasm. Even without that preview, I could predict a future for them on stages other than a rock. I'm not sure about their song, though.

> I like my beans and berries.
> They are so de—li—cious.

Mabel sings the first syllable, Sibel the second, and they harmonize on the third. They have perfect pitch. At this point, Willie crawls out of the pool and groans.

"Bear! Please come save me from this."

The girls ignore him and sing on.

I eat my beans and berries.
They are so nu—tri—tious
And give me all those good things
Like vi—ta—mins and pro—te—ins
To make me big and strong.
That's why I sing this song.
Beans and berries, beans and berries,
That's how I get that in—gre—di—ent
Called an an—ti—ox—i—dent.

Tommy yells from the pool. "What the heck is an an-ti-ox-i-dent?"

Sibel chants: "It's in the berries."

In unison: "It keeps you healthy."

I don't know who wrote the song, but for sure it wasn't Paul McCartney. Bless their little hearts, they rehearsed it every day after school. It has a routine of dance steps based on the Hannah Montana movies that they've seen numerous times. MTV would love a video of this performance in the sun; the spectacular, sparkling waterfall in the background; their sweet, young voices accompanied by the music of water rushing down the mountain. During postadventure exposure, a TV anchor asks whether it's true that they stood on a rock in the middle of the forest, chased by kidnappers and a six-hundred-pound bear, and sang about nutrition.

"Yes, we did," they answer in unison, almond eyes flashing.

"Can you sing it for me now?" the anchor asks. Gotta love these girls because they jump up and belt it out while performing some of the dance steps. That gets them an agent who has "Beans and Berries" professionally arranged. Now that would be a challenge for any musician. But who knows? Nutrition is a hot subject. Everyone's writing about it. It could become a big hit. Stranger songs have struck it big. After "It's Tough out Here for a Pimp," anything is possible.

I am reminded, however, that music in the Dimension is quite different. Earth's scale has eight notes. Do-re-mi-fa-so-la-ti-do. Our scale has hundreds of notes, and we use them to communicate. It's a language of unlimited harmonious melodies that energize the intellect and increase mental capacity. Creativity surges. Conversations become glorious symphonies. Earlier, I referred to the understanding of time and space. Well, the use of music as language is what made that possible. We could say the Dimension "rocks" with it. I hope that someday humans will hear it too. It's entirely possible that dogs already hear it.

But while earth music is not as profound or intellectual, the twins' voices are sweet to everyone except Willie. He clamps his hands over his ears and jumps back in the pool. The others applaud the performance, and YoYo joins with some *arfs*. Willie challenges Tommy and Scotty to see how long they can stay under water. Tommy wins, although he almost drowns, and Willie switches his attention to the girls.

"The water is great. C'mon in."

They know the invitation smacks of more "Willie" pranks, and they decline.

"We'll wait for you to get out, thank you."

After all the risks and dangers of the day, this is a chance to play and just be children. Willie paddles around the pool splashing Tommy and Scotty while he moves closer to the crashing water. Closer and closer … it looks like he's going under it. Yes. Willie swims into the waterfall and disappears. Vickie knows her brother is a daredevil who loves to take risks, but now she is terrified for him.

"Help! Help! Willie is drowning."

Kevin responds by diving into the pool.

"Willie! Willie!" Vickie continues to scream.

"I'm here," he calmly answers, peering at them through the falling water. "I'm here. Inside a cave. A big one."

Oh my word. Not another cave. I've had all the caves I can take.

"Willie, you get back down here right now," Vickie scolds her mischievous brother. YoYo, sensing trouble, hops to her side.

"Okay, here I come."

Goodness! He jumped directly into the waterfall. Even I was scared for a moment, but, thank heaven, he popped up in the pool and laughed as if he had played a joke on us. They paddle to the edge. Above, there is that whirring sound again. The helicopter has returned.

While they wave and shout, "We're here! We're here!" Katy, who was on watch duty, runs down with bad news.

"They're coming. The men are coming. They're in the woods below us. They'll get here before the helicopter sees us."

"Where can we go?" they ask each other.

"We can hide in there." Willie points to the waterfall. He jumps in without waiting for them to agree. Moments later, he's on a ledge.

"Come on! Hurry up! This is perfect. We'll be safe in here."

Katy jumps in and drags Scotty and Tommy with her. Vickie holds her nose, grabs Chrissie, and leaps in. Kevin pulls the hand-holding, resisting twins in and floats on his back to guide them under the waterfall. Once again these kids are stuck in a cave. I tag along, of course. In fact, I linger under the downpour. Tons of water pound through my space. It is quite a sensation, reminding me of a visit to Epsilon Aurigae in the constellation Auriga. I know I shouldn't name-drop or brag about going to the hottest destination spot in the universe. Everyone wants to go there. But I never did any cool stuff on Earth. Even the Celestials know I have a lot of catching up to do.

Dripping wet and shaking with fear, they look for the men through a curtain of water. They don't see them. But they do see Lucky—sitting on a rock by the pool. They forgot about him. They left him alone to face the men. Guilt overtakes them. But YoYo still has me—perched on his back. And he is a survivor, so, YoYo, let's see what these guys are up to and figure out how we can take them down. Hmmm? A stub of a tail *rat-a-tat-tats* a response. It's game on.

José and Adolpho picked up the children's trail in the woods, but it wasn't easy for them. They aren't used to hiking or tracking through forests. Not that I'm sympathetic. Greed kept them going—fantasies about a million-dollar ransom. They are tired and thirsty from the trek. The waterfall looks like an oasis to them. But the helicopter flies overhead and forces them to retreat into the woods. It circles, hovers over the waterfall, and flies off. The men move out.

The helicopter pilot, Captain Dave Henderson, reports: "Arrow Wing to command center. Covered the area and no sign of kids. Funny, though. A little dog is sitting by the waterfall. Alone. Nobody's around."

A familiar voice asks, "A kind of terrier dog?"

It's that Captain MacDonald. What's he doing at the command center? Seems like if there's action, he finds a way to get in the middle of it.

"Affirmative. It's barking at something in the woods, but I can't see anything, and there's no place to set down. I'll circle again."

"Roger. All the search teams are on the way, so stand by." He turns to Officer Bonner. "You might as well notify Mrs. Hancock. We found YoYo. The dog's gotta be YoYo. I can't wait to hear the whole story—it's going to be a good one, for sure. We need to get a doctor—to treat dog bites."

I want to be there when Holly hears that.

Chapter Eighteen

YoYo doesn't know José and Adolpho, but the nose that detects chemicals tells him these guys are dangerous. They have bad intentions. YoYo still looks like a train wreck, but his ears are up, teeth are bared. That's about as ferocious as a five-pound terrier can get. With the *aaarrrffff … aaarrrrfffff … aaarrrrrfrrff* bark, he warns them—dares them to come closer. Adolpho is huge, with arms and legs the size of tree trunks. He's carefree about approaching YoYo, bounding right to the pool. A *little* dog. That works better for YoYo. He launches a surprise attack on Adolpho's ankle—a quick bite, but teeth penetrate. Adolpho is annoyed and kicks at the dog. YoYo sidesteps and leaps at him. Jaws snap, and teeth pierce a giant, muscled calf.

"Ouch," Adolpho cries.

The dummy doesn't get the message that these furry five pounds represent a serious adversary. José thinks a little dog biting a big tough guy is funny and chuckles as Adolpho grimaces and pulls up his pant leg. When he sees the damage—blood running down his leg—he explodes, cursing and cursing more. The curses are omitted here, according to the rules.

José is tall and thin. He has to bend over the pool to get a drink. Just the kind of opportunity YoYo can't pass up. He likes biting butts even more than soft tummies. Little fangs cut like scissors into the skinny behind and hit bone. José screams. Now it's Adolpho's turn to laugh. But José doesn't think it's funny and retaliates with a good kick. YoYo issues a seamless stream of *woorrffff … wooorrrfffs*, objecting to such abuse. But while he makes a smooth move backward to dodge the kick, a big foot lands on him, and he's tossed into the air. He falls to the ground with a thud and doesn't move. Behind the curtain of falling water, the horrified children watch.

Katy whispers, "Oh no. No. This can't be happening to Lucky again."

"It's our fault too. We forgot about him. He wanted to protect us and look what they did to him."

"Did they kill him?" Chrissie asks.

"No, honey. You just wait. Lucky will be okay."

"Hey, right." A doubtful Scotty shakes his head.

Katy, he wasn't just protecting you. He told those guys off in no uncertain dog language. Those *wooorrrffff*s sent a tough message. Unfortunately, it's not appropriate to include it in this report. My advice: don't write off any dog who has a vocabulary like that.

Kevin doesn't want to sound negative, but while he likes Lucky a lot, he realizes that the dog can give away their hiding place.

"Yeah, and those guys are pretty stupid if they don't figure out that if the dog's still here, we must be too."

They ignore him. "Go, Lucky, go," they whisper as Kevin heads into the dark cave behind them.

Bats, disturbed from their slumber, fly over his head, fluttering their wings with quick, repetitive pulses that bounce off the walls and guide them safely through the cave.

Kevin stumbles over rocks as the cave gets darker and narrower. He knows it can go for miles into the mountain, and he'll never find a way out. Just when he's ready to give up, a ray of sunlight streams into the cave. It comes from an opening between some big rocks. He pushes at one, but it doesn't move. He uses all his strength to shove as hard as he can. The rock moves an inch. He shoves again. Another inch. He's exhausted, and his shoulders hurt, but he thrusts again and again, and finally the rock tumbles out. Light floods in, blinding him.

Blinking, he sees a green meadow below that stretches for miles. A perfect hiding place until the helicopter comes back. Suddenly I remember the peek I had at this child's future. He expects to follow in Dad's footsteps and become a scientist, but after this, there is a new direction—a major in forestry. He does seem quite at home here in the woods. He has risen to all the challenges. Definitely a born leader who one day will manage this huge park. Kind of ironic, but he sure knows an awful lot about it.

Not knowing he's in for a life in the very park from which he wants to escape, Kevin moves back through the cave and finds the group still intent on watching Lucky harassing the men who want to rest by the pool and consider their options. They think they finished YoYo off, but he has revived and, although a little woozy, interrupts them with weak *arfs* that they try to ignore.

"Hola, José, maybe we should give up, go back, and collect from Hector. If we don't catch the kids, we end up with nothin'."

"You crazy, amigo? You think I went through all this for nothin'? We're gonna get those kids. Once we got 'em, they gotta give us money to get them back—big money. See that dog? It didn't get here by itself. It's their dog. That means they're around here somewhere. Now where could they hide?"

Adolpho laughs and leans over the pool.

"Yeah, maybe they're in the water. You see kids in there, José?"

José looks thoughtfully into the deep water, up at the waterfall, then at Adolpho. They exchange knowing looks. Adolpho raises his eyebrows.

"You think?"

"I'll bet."

I'll pass on that one. Why waste time counting a mere vice like betting for a guy like José?

Preparing to go into the water, he removes a shoe. YoYo takes notice. He sees an easy target and sneaks a quick bite at a heel. José swats him away with a curse.

"You, again, you little *so-and-so*." [Words subbed.] "I thought I finished you off. You want another good kick in the head?"

YoYo responds with a steady stream of irritating *rrrooouuuffs*.

"This dog is like a cat. I thought I got 'em good, but he's back."

"So kick him again."

"Yeah. You kick him, if ya can. I'm checking this out."

"I don't swim, so I'll stay here," Adolpho confesses.

The truth is he's too macho to admit that water terrifies him.

Both men are unaware of the threat lurking on the rocks above. It watches them, nose in the air, inhaling their scents. Well, well. It's our favorite bear. It picked up their tracks and followed them. These are his woods—his territory. These invaders will be dealt with in bear terms. Except there is a game-changer. Barking reverberates on the rocks. The bear pauses to listen. These are familiar sounds that bring back memories of a previous humiliating encounter. The men are replaced. The bear has a new objective: a tasty snack and revenge.

YoYo smelled it before the men saw it. Bears do have a rank scent. Strong vapors precede them and announce their presence. Ears flat against his head, nose quivering, and tail between his legs, YoYo scampers to the opposite side. José doesn't get the odor, but he does see the animal and yells, "Bear!" He flees to the other side of the pool and jumps on the rocks. Adolpho doesn't understand the problem until the bear is so close, he hears panting. When he looks up, the bear is almost on him. He races to join José on the rocks. The bear pursues them. José hurls himself into the water. Adolpho hesitates.

"Get in," José commands, splashing toward the waterfall.

"I can't swim."

"Just kick your legs," José instructs.

Adolpho plunges in, disappears, and then pops up, kicking wildly to stay afloat.

"Go to the waterfall," José spits out along with a mouthful of water. "We'll be safe there, amigo."

Oh yeah? The dummies don't know that bears are good swimmers. This one fearlessly plunges into the water and expertly paddles after them. YoYo watches with interest from his catbird seat. His jaws are closed, lips are open, cheeks are high, and his eyelids drop. I see his lower teeth. Guess what? He's smiling. Yup! I know a smile when I see one, even if it is on a dog.

In the cave, the kids watch the men move toward the waterfall.

"They're on the way in here ... if they make it. We can't wait to see what happens ... we've got to go. Follow me," Kevin tells the group.

For the second time that day, the kids crawl through darkness and dirt, once again scared, but more terrified of the threat behind them.

The bear closes in on the men.

José says, "Amigo, this ain't workin'. I'm getting out."

He detours to the side of the pool, crawls out, and runs into the woods with a slight disadvantage. He's missing a shoe. Adolpho follows but also has trouble. His shoes are full of water. The bear easily clambers out of the pool and catches up to them. They hear it panting close behind. They also hear *aaafff … aaafff … aaafff.* It's YoYo, and he has a strategic advantage—his very special dog nose that lets him run, bark, and breathe—all at the same time. And he can keep this up indefinitely. It will drive the bear mad. If that seems like small change, imagine a 5,000-meter race in the Olympics with runners singing their national anthems all the way to the finish line. Besides, the bear has a lesson to learn. Never run from a predator—a lion, a tiger, or YoYo unless you want to be chased. He's on the bear's heels. I wonder which one is David and which is Goliath.

"Climb a tree," José instructs.

Easy to say, but these are towering sycamores. They dodge between them until Adolpho finds a tree with low branches. He grabs one and pulls himself up. José scrambles to join him. They climb higher into the tree. I can't believe this. Don't they know that bears climb trees about as easily as monkeys? But they get lucky. The bear stops to wait for the "predator" racing toward him. YoYo turned up the throttle to catch up, and now he has to put on the brakes to keep from careening into his "prey." He slides past him in the dirt. The bear smacks its lips, tasting the snack in front of him. But the "snack" roars at the bear. I don't need a spectrograph analysis to know that the volume is at least 130 decibels … proof of a recovery from near death that not even a visit to Lourdes could accomplish. And what I heard was not the wolf bark. When I said he roared at the bear, I did mean a roar. A lion's roar.

His head is up, jaw is dropped. Expelling air from his lungs, YoYo coughs out a steady stream of vibrating *aaauuuuuuoooffff … aaaoouuuooooff … aaaoouuufffffffffooooooos.* Well, I said I wouldn't mind a lot of vowels. But how on earth did he ever learn to imitate a lion? Did the Committee's program mix things up a bit? Dogs do mimic each other's barks, but what I'm hearing doesn't resemble a bark. Maybe he heard a lion on the PBS *Nature* programs that Holly watches, created his own version of a roar, and added it to his repertoire. I wouldn't put anything past him. Or the Committee.

Unfortunately, the bear isn't scared. It's annoyed, and it charges. YoYo strategically retreats into a convenient foxhole. The bear reaches into the hole. YoYo sees the giant claw coming and snaps. Oops. Somebody just found a bear toe in his mouth. Somebody who's hungry. Somebody who hasn't eaten all day. This toe could take the edge off. He chews, but it's not the roast chicken that Holly gives him. He spits it out. The bear, not wanting to risk another toe, turns back to the men, and easily swings up into the tree. The desperate men kick at claws that lash out at them. José foolishly says, "Scoot, go away." About as effective as telling a teenager to be home by ten o'clock.

YoYo emerges from the hole, this time doing the bark-rant: *rrrrooouuufff ... rrrooouuuffff ... rrrooouuuffff*—the sound that's supposed to irritate. But it's too weak, and the bear glides down the tree as if it were a pole. YoYo wisely retreats to safety, and the bear climbs back into the tree. The men struggle to avoid the dangerously close claws. Both men and bear grunt a lot. But again, YoYo saves them. Stationed at the base of the tree, he calls the bear to come down and fight like ... I was going to say "a man," but this time YoYo better be a little more politically correct. And right now, I'm not sure how to translate those *rrrooouuuffff*s, so they're added to my ever-expanding list for further analysis.

Scientific researchers admit that dog barks have meaning, even if they don't understand them. What's encouraging to us is that the process that produces barks is the same process that produces human speech—vibrations in the vocal cords and the air that flows through those cords. What comes out of the mouth is either a bark or speech. I hope that's not too technical, but it does lead back to the basic question: Is it possible that camouflaged in those *rrroouufff*s we'll discover words? English, of course. It's a reasonable question, and I'm hopeful that the answer will be positive.

We have an unexpected development. It seems that YoYo's routine wore the bear out. When bears are tired, they take a nap, wherever they are. This bear curls up into a smelly ball at the base of the tree. Not a bad strategy to prevent an escape while he takes a snooze. Loud snores bring YoYo out to investigate. He uses the opportunity to check every inch of the bear. He checks a bleeding foot minus a toe. The tail is of great interest. His sniffing nose investigates the bear everywhere. I won't go into detail, but when he has finished, he knows just about everything about the bear. And probably more than he wants to know.

While the bear sleeps, Adolpho leans onto a wide branch.

"José, I been thinking."

"What about, amigo?"

"I been thinking it's funny about Hector. He made a lot of trips for us and always delivered. I think he ran because he was scared of us."

"Why should he be scared of us? We have a deal. When we collect, we pay."

"But that's what I wonder. What if he knew we couldn't collect."

"Why not?"

"Maybe because he didn't have the shipment. Maybe because somebody took it. Maybe somebody got there before we did. He was there, wasn't he? He wouldn't have been there if he didn't have something to deliver."

"Amigo, you think too much."

"And I wonder who would know our schedule for the pickup."

Adolpho is interrupted when the refreshed bear wakes, stands on his hind legs, growls, and claws at the tree trunk like it's a warm-up. A sudden leap thrusts the massive body into the tree. The animal climbs to José's branch, close enough to reach out at him. Adolpho moves farther away on his branch. The bear sinks a claw into José. Long nails drag through his flesh. It hurts like the devil, and he screams for Adolpho to help him. But Adolpho watches in silence and makes no effort to help him. Instead, he asks the big question: "Who would know, José, besides the two of us?"

Chapter Nineteen

"The bats are okay," Willie soothes the kids, who freak out as hundreds of the creatures swarm over their heads in the cave. "They're headed out to dinner. Anyway, we're way too big to be featured on a bat menu." The kids chuckle at that—you can count on Willie. They reach the big rock and see the gorgeous meadow. But it's upstaged by a helicopter in the distance. They scream and wave to attract attention.

"Let's build a fire. They'll see the smoke. 'Cuz I wanna get outta here." Tommy is not alone. They all want to go home. Willie does his Boy Scout thing again.

The pilot spots the smoke and flies toward it. Nine happy faces appear, the boys in their jockeys, the girls in bras and bikinis. The tiny tot waves and cheers.

"Are you okay?" the pilot asks, using a microphone.

They nod and laugh in response.

"Control. This is Arrow Wing. Made contact. Nine. All look intact."

"Control to Arrow Wing. Hallelujah! And congratulations. Can you pick them up?"

"Negative. There's no place to land. They're on a precipice."

"National Guard is closest. ETA approximately forty-five minutes. Can you stay in the area until the rescue is completed?"

"Affirmative. Will keep children in view. FYI, all smiling. Look happy. But dirty. Very dirty. All in underwear."

"Even the tot?"

"No. The little one has some kind of a dress."

"Good. That will make Mac happy."

"Right. 10-40 Henderson. Over and out."

Captain Henderson maneuvers as low as possible. "A rescue team is on the way. Stay where you are."

The kids plunk down on the rocks to wait, and they watch the helicopter slowly circle around them.

At the control center, cheers erupt with the news. The captain collapses into a chair and mops his face with a handkerchief before anyone sees his tears, muttering, "Thank God, thank God she's safe." Whatever else he may be, on this score, he's real. Maybe he's not a phony. Well—maybe not totally phony, and maybe I have to do a reevaluation. Anyone can change ... overcome bad habits, right? Like me, I hope.

When Holly got the call from Officer Bonner that they had found YoYo, she immediately left for the command center. I understand how elated she is, how relieved she must be, but I wish she didn't try to break the sound barrier. I admit I'm not one to speak about speeding. She arrives in time to hear that the kids are safe. She assumes that YoYo is with them and has no idea that, at this moment, he's watching the bear attack José and Adolpho. With some satisfaction, I might add.

Ed Hodges, the reporter from ABC, spots her and points the microphone at her. "Aren't you the owner of the lost dog?"

From the look Holly gives him, I don't have to get inside her head to know what she's thinking.

Here we go again. Just when things had settled down to normal! Now the phones will ring nonstop, and people will knock on the door and ask to take pictures of YoYo. And they call him Demon Dog. He is not a demon. He's a little sweetheart, a playful puppy—who happens to be very protective. That's the only thing that makes him different from every other five-pound Yorkshire terrier in the world.

"We don't know for sure it was YoYo, but he did run away. He pulled off his collar to chase a cat on that street. YoYo likes children and loves to play, so it's possible that he followed them on the bus."

Ed persists. "Are you aware of the team of doctors ready to treat the dog bites the children are expected to have?"

Holly recoils as if a rattlesnake bit her. "What? You must be kidding. Who's trying to turn YoYo into a villain who would hurt children? You just wait until you talk to the children. You'll be sorry if you accuse YoYo of biting. I know YoYo. Do you know that he foiled a bank robbery? Do you know that he—"

She stops in time, remembering that the episode with the terrorists is classified information. She turns away. Good for her. Then she turns back.

"You're going to be sorry you said that," she says and stomps off.

Chapter Twenty

Rescue teams are on the way. The hovering helicopter makes the kids feel secure. But one thing bothers them. Lucky is missing.

"I hope Lucky escaped the bear and those men."

"Yeah. Three against one little dog is unfair."

"I wonder who he belongs to. I'll bet someone is really upset that he got lost."

"Hey, that little dog's a tiger. If the bear got him, I betcha he gave it a hard time."

"Sooo, isn't he some kind of a terrier? I thought terriers were supposed to kill rats."

Willie is the dog expert. "I think he's a Yorkshire terrier or maybe a Silky. Definitely not a Cairn. Cairn terriers can weigh seventy pounds, and I doubt if Lucky weighs more than five or six pounds. Anyway, Lucky isn't fussy. If he doesn't like you, you're toast."

Willie has studied all the dog breeds because his goal is to have a dog. Every day he Googles AKC sites and looks at rescue sites to shop for his future dog. His mom promised him he could get a dog if he improves his grades. She's not too happy about it, though—she's sure she'll end up with most of the responsibility—but she agreed because she wants him to qualify for a scholarship at a good college. Since the deal was made, he does his homework before he watches TV. We're waiting on the grades. Now I understand why he has so many dogs in his future.

Katy adds, "Have you noticed how Chrissie talks to him? She carries him around, cuddles him, talks to him. He's like a little baby until he goes into action."

"Yeah, then watch out."

"Some little kids are afraid of dogs."

"Well, Chrissie and Lucky have a mutual pact. She hugs him, and he protects her."

"Oh, he protects all of us." Katy always gets in a good word about YoYo. She really likes dogs. And she has lots of them in her future because she's going to be a veterinarian. She and Willie will have lots in common. But romance blooms between Katy and Kevin. Well, we saw it all start here, didn't we? The beginning of a strong bond? Yup! There's a forty-year anniversary in store for them.

It's fun to think what I could do if I could really use this information. And I already read minds. I could open a business. And advertise, "Come one, come all, angel tells fortunes."

Angela, Angela. What are we going to do with you? Why can't you behave like an angel?

I apologize profusely.

I'm so, so sorry. Honestly, Committee, I just don't know what comes over me.

I reassure them with a promise to be the best angel on the block. I have to. They're watching.

The twins listen to the group discuss YoYo, but they don't participate. They have their own communication system of secret codes. When a decision has been made, they nod at each other. This one looks serious, and they burst out, "We love Lucky. We want Lucky to be our dog."

Chrissie reacts. "No! My dog! Lucky my dog!"

Little Chrissie. She can be assertive. Now it would be easy to predict that, with exposure, agents, model agencies, and Hollywood will beckon once they spot that sweet face on the news and even on magazine covers. The snooping expedition showed that she does grow into a great beauty, but on the inside, she is caring and nurturing—perhaps not the best fit for showbiz. So the surprise is that she doesn't go Hollywood. She does the unpredictable and becomes a nurse. I love it. Imagine a sick person waking from a coma and seeing that face. He'll think he's seeing an angel. Yeah. If only we all looked like that. Anyway, Chrissie's in for a nice surprise. Her father got an emergency leave and is flying back from Afghanistan. He'll be there to greet her when she gets home.

A large black bird soars overhead and circles above them. They watch, fascinated, as a California raven, four-foot wings flapping, navigates down and lands near them. The raven is one of the most intelligent birds, capable of a wide variety of sounds, and it can even imitate humans. Once again we're in for some entertainment. Tommy throws a seed pod, and with a "cronk-cronk-cronk," the bird hops to pick it up. A sharp beak flips the pod back at Tommy. They kids laugh. I knew they could have fun with a raven.

"Hey, the bird wants to play ball with you."

Tommy tosses the pod back with a "See if you can catch this."

The bird meets the pod in midair and bounces it up several times. Soccer practice? The bird scoops up the pod, lands, and with sharp, metallic "tock tock tocks," tears it open. Seeds disappear down a shaggy, iridescent-purple throat. Scotty throws another one, saying, "Hey, bird." The bird responds with a deep croaking that sounds like "Hey, bird," and skips toward him.

"The bird is talking! The bird is talking."

"Hey, bird, hey bird," they all cry. The raven answers with its own version of "Hey, bird," and then, of all things, does a somersault in front of them. The kids laugh and enjoy the show while the raven croaks a "ha-ha-ha" that sounds like their laugher and performs another somersault. They clap for the performance, and I swear that bird stands straight up and takes a bow. Then it gleefully bounces up and down. Scotty falls on the ground giggling uncontrollably. I should take a look and see what's in store for the little guy. Here he is at age thirteen and not so little anymore. Still bashful, with freckles, but he's also 6'1" and still growing. Not so unusual, either. Ernest Hemingway was 5'7" at sixteen and then grew an inch a month for the next six months. On his sixteenth birthday, Scotty will measure 6'7". Here comes the grand finale: he becomes a big basketball star. The one they'll call "Little Scotty."

Who's future did I miss? Vickie and Tommy. Do I have time for another sneak peek? Why stop now … Uh-oh. The big door has a padlock on it. They know. No more peeks for me. From behind the door, I hear an irritated grumble. "Youngsters—you can't control them."

"Patience," a gentle voice responds. "We have to wait for them to mature."

It's been a long time since I was caught with my hand in the cookie jar. This time, I didn't get a spanking. But then we wouldn't expect "Spare the rod and spoil the child" from them, and patience probably works better up here than it does down there. Anyway, now the door into the future is shut tight, and I see that the helicopter pilot is signaling the children. He points down the mountain, and they race to the edge. Below, a group of soldiers climb toward them. The raven, disappointed to lose its audience, complains with testy cronk-cronk-cronks and flies to a nearby tree to watch the action.

"Hello, hello," the soldiers shout. The children wave and scream, delirious with joy. A TV reporter embedded with the rescue team turns his camera on to capture the scene. Images of nine children flying into the arms of the National Guard go out to the millions who anxiously waited for news of their rescue.

After the jubilant greeting, jackets are handed out, and the children quickly slip them on. The sergeant in charge inspects them for injuries or problems. They were prepared to take the youngsters out on stretchers.

"Are these scratches from the dog?" the sergeant asks Scotty.

"Hey, you don't mean Lucky, do you? No, these are from the thicket. We had to crawl through all the thorns to get inside."

"The dog didn't bite you?"

Nine children speak in unison. "No. He saved us."

A sincere four-year-old adds, "He's the bestest dog there ever was."

"Good. Then you don't have to go on the stretchers. We'll carry you out."

The sergeant kneels and tells Willie to climb on his back.

"Whatayamean?" Willie asks.

He can't believe that after all he has been through, they want to humiliate him.

"You want to carry me out like a baby?" he protests.

One of the soldiers picks him up and settles him on the sergeant's back.

"What's your name, son?"

"Willie Williams."

"Well, Willie, this is no time to be a hero. You've done enough already. In fact, how you kids made it this far is awesome. Now you just relax, and let us do our jobs. It's our job to bring you back, you know. We can't take a chance and let anything happen to you. You understand?"

Willie negotiates. "Will you let me down before we get there so I can at least walk the last part?"

"Sure 'nuff."

I saw quite a few Broadway plays in my lifetime, and I can truthfully say that not one ever contained more drama than the emotional rescue of those children, which millions viewed. In living rooms throughout the country, tears flow and goose bumps abound. YouTube will run the video forever.

"Let's go," the sergeant calls, and the trek through the forest begins. The children call repeatedly for Lucky.

"Lucky, Lucky, where are you?"

"C'mere, Lucky. Good dog. C'mere."

The twins harmonize: "Lluuukkeeeeee, Lluukkkeeee, Lluuuukkkkeeeeeee."

Even the solders call for him, but YoYo can't answer. He's still working.

The soldiers hear the stories about the waterfall, the cave behind it, and the scary bats that flew over their heads. But there is no mention of the tunnel. Perhaps it's too traumatizing for them to describe.

"Hey, I'm hungry," Scotty announces. "I could eat a whole pizza."

That's the cue for the twins to begin the pizza song. There are lots of variations, mostly commercial, but the children learned this one in kindergarten. The lyrics conjure up the flavors of tomatoes, cheese, onions and mushrooms until even an angel finds herself salivating.

Now all the children are singing. Even the soldiers pick up on the pizza song. Viewers love it, and pizza parlors get the message. Soon the highway is jammed with their delivery trucks. Ice cream trucks follow. The kids are in for a big, well-deserved treat.

When they approach the center, Willie cries, "Let me down! Let me down! You promised!"

Hand in hand with their rescuers, nine kids march into the center where the families wait. Holly is there too, looking for YoYo.

Captain MacDonald sprints to Chrissie and scoops her up in his arms, unashamed of the relieved tears that flow. Photographers rush to capture the moment. Amy is right behind him. Chrissie cries, "Mama," and little arms reach for her mother. Vickie and Willie run to the sobbing Mrs. Williams and throw their arms around her.

"It's okay, Ma. We're okay."

Mrs. Hansen releases her children from big hugs to study them. She expects to find them depressed and upset. Instead, they are full of energy with idiotically happy smiles on their faces. These kids define the word *resilient*. The twins are disappointed—no parents to greet them—until they see a familiar face. Tiny as she is, Lupe picks the twins up and holds them for a long time, crying, "My prayers were answered."

Mr. Cohen envelopes Kevin in a tight embrace. "How are you, son?"

"Good, Dad, it turned out great except we lost Lucky."

"Lucky?"

"The dog who saved us. More than once."

Holly asks the captain in a loud, panicky voice, "Where's YoYo? Where's YoYo? You said he was with them. But where is he? What happened to him? Please, where is my dog?"

"Granpa, I have a dog," Chrissie announces.

The captain stares at her. "What do you mean, you have a dog?"

"Yes, Granpa. I love him. He's so cute. I give him kisses, and he kisses me back."

The captain wonders: *Hmmm. The dog doesn't sound like Demon Dog—YoYo. And the doctors didn't find any bites on the children. I wonder if it wasn't …*

"Well, Mrs. Hancock," the captain confesses, "Chrissie's dog doesn't sound like YoYo. It couldn't have been him on the bus. I made a mistake."

Kevin interrupts to ask Holly, "Is your dog a very small, brown and black terrier?"

"Yes, and he answers to the name of YoYo."

"YoYo? YoYo? What did I tell you?" Katy exclaims. "No wonder he always came back. Lucky is a yo-yo." She gestures with her hands to show how a yo-yo works.

"We named him Lucky. Then he died. After that, we lost him, 'cause he ran after a bear. That's the last time we saw him."

"Wait a minute, wait a minute ..." The captain is incredulous.

"Did you say he chased a bear? Is that what you said?" Holly doesn't want to believe this.

The children all speak at once. It's so garbled, even I have a hard time unscrambling it. Each child rattles off the story of how Lucky came to their aid so many times ... about all the adventures they had. The families, officers, reporters, move in to hear this story. Mind you, this scene is being sent out live on TV, radio, even the Internet. Maybe the whole world is hearing about the dog the Committee selected for this mission. Millions of dogs were available—former police dogs, guard dogs, seeing-eye dogs, strong German shepherds or Great Danes, clever hunting dogs—but YoYo is the one they selected. An example of unintended consequences? Or was there some foreknowledge—a plan for YoYo in all of this?

Well, I've always loved a mystery. Evidence that YoYo can form some words is inconclusive, but it is true that he's responsible for saving nine children. Maybe the Committee's real objective will never be revealed to me, but one thing is for sure: It worked out well for everyone except for the bad guys. They broke the rule. I always tried to abide by the Ten Commandments, but somehow that very simple oath—Do no harm—was really easy for me to live by.

"Okay, okay, okay," the captain tells them. "Chrissie, now we know for sure your Lucky couldn't have been this lady's dog. YoYo's crazy, but not crazy enough to chase a bear."

"The best part is when Kevin saved Chrissie," Vickie offers. "She cried a lot, but she was okay as long as she had Lucky ... her best friend."

The captain is speechless. Oh, I love this.

"Are you saying that my dog, YoYo, helped you, protected you?" Holly believes that Lucky is YoYo, and for her, it's payback time. She wants the captain to hear the answer.

"That's just half the story. There's more," Kevin offers while his dad glows with pride. "A lot more."

"But I want to know, where is YoYo now?"

"We left him at the waterfall. He attacked those two guys—oh my gosh, you should have seen how he went after them, even though he was so weak he could hardly stand. Then the bear chased him."

"It ate Lucky," the twins cry.

"I'll bet on Lucky." Atta girl, Katy. With YoYo, you're holding a royal flush. "Can't somebody go find him?"

Holly turns to the captain. She doesn't have to say a word.

"Get another team out to look for the dog—whatever the darned thing's name is."

At this point, I think it's safe to say the captain has learned a lesson: Bad intentions can backfire. For some reason, they usually do. If there is any doubt, these pages should offer some proof. So the captain won't try to manipulate any more dogs to further his career. The good news for him is that I am absolutely sure he won't have to ... because he'll win the election. I don't know much about politics, but I know when voters see the photograph of him with Chrissie, they'll see a man they didn't know before. This is a good man, a man with a loving heart. That's invaluable in politics. I can't get behind the door to confirm it, but I predict he'll be the next district attorney.

Other teams continue to search for the men. While there's still some light, Captain Henderson makes another trip to survey the forest and waterfall. But the hardest part is over. The children are safe. They demolish lots of pizzas and put a huge dent in the supply of ice cream, especially the chocolate fudge. With full tummies, they are ready to head for home with their families. The director, what's his name—Hal Brocklehurst—shows up and utters just one phrase to Captain MacDonald: "Déjà-vu?"

In other words, eat crow, Captain.

Chapter Twenty-One

In a whirlwind of activity, the center is crowded with officers, soldiers, and reporters eager to get the story out. One news anchor for TIVE-TV, Karen Cotter, sneaks off into the woods with her cameraman. That's curious, so naturally I follow to see what she's up to. Oh, she wants to do a summary without any interruptions. Her approach is the standard talking heads routine. In the background, two cars—one the squad car that got stuck in the mud—are parked among the trees.

She opens with, "Ladies and gentlemen, you have witnessed the telling of one of the most dramatic tales of our time."

I think there are some unintended additions to the scene because … a door of the car in the background is slowly opening … Is it what I think it is? This may get interesting as the action continues. A foot emerges from the door and hangs in the air. Now another foot. Feet continue to back out of the car and reveal legs attached to the feet. Legs drop onto knees that crawl out from behind the door of the car. Lo and behold, what do we see but the backside of none other than Hector Santos. I know it's him. Who else would have burned pants and exposed pink flesh?

He must have observed Karen and company from the backseat, felt they were too close for comfort, and decided to leave his hiding place. He has no idea the car is in camera range. Karen's audience must wonder what the strange activity is. The cameraman wonders too, and while Karen talks about the kidnapping, he zooms in for a close-up. He gets a full-screen image of a red, badly blistered, chubby rear end. "Bingo," he declares and stays focused as viewers gasp but remain glued to the TV to watch the figure crawl toward a thick grove of cottonwoods about fifteen feet away. No bathroom intermissions. The network doesn't break for a commercial. This is just too precious.

What exactly are Hector's intentions? Does he actually think he can hide in the woods until they leave and then sneak back to the car? The area is crawling with police. He can't be that optimistic. Or stupid. We watch him pause to take out a cell phone, enter a number, and dial. His expression says, "No luck. Dead batteries," and he tucks it away, wincing in pain with every movement as blisters break open. His mouth forms a silent, agonized scream. I can't help it—I empathize with him. It's gotta hurt.

A cop enters the scene headed toward the squad car, and the cameraman adjusts the focus to include him. Hector hears footsteps, and we see him tense up and peer under the car. What's he going to do now? The officer gets in the driver's seat, and Hector scrambles toward the safety of the trees. He doesn't see a second cop walk to the squad car and open the passenger door. He turns to get in and spots our fugitive. Moving stealthily, he creeps up on Hector. It is only when the cop stands over him and says, "Well, well, well. What have we here?" that Hector learns that he's been discovered. The cop calls his partner, "Hey, Joe, c'mere and see what's turned up."

Hector streams a series of excuses at them. "I was going to the bathroom. I have to go. I go to woods …" His excuses fall on deaf ears.

"Oh, yeah, and would you mind telling me how you got that bullet wound on your shoulder and how you … uh … lost the back of your pants and your skin along with them?"

"Bad dog. Bad dog. I try to save children, and he push me into fire. I want to help children from gang—"

"Uhh huhhh! That's not the way we heard it."

The camera moves in again when the officers handcuff Hector and drag him to the car. All the while, he's jabbering, "I didn't do it … I didn't know the kids were on the bus … I wouldn't hurt any kids …" His bottom hits the seat, and he screams, "They were going to kill me. Somebody stole the drugs from me."

The officers offer no sympathy, but in a way, I do feel kind of sorry for him. Maybe because he's not very bright. He didn't know the most basic thing: there are consequences for breaking the rule.

Ironically, Karen Cotter is unaware of the drama behind her. She concludes her report: "They have yet to capture the man who stole the school bus."

Fifteen minutes later, after the children identify Hector, Karen is back on the air, gloating that they have an exclusive: The capture of the culprit. Talk about being at the right place at the right time! Here's another prediction: That lucky, accidental scoop will make her famous. That's how so many stars are born—accidental, lucky breaks—on Earth, but not in the Dimension. We know only too well how stars are formed in the endless heavens. Our home.

Captain MacDonald takes stock: "One down, two to go. Or three, if we include YoYo."

Yes, Captain, please, don't forget him. I need to finish my report. I am hopeful because the helicopter skims over the woods and circles the waterfall. Now it hovers over the sixty-foot sycamores. Captain Henderson dips it quite low so he can see through the branches.

Is there something in that tree? Yes, it's a man ... a big guy, hanging on to a branch. Uh-oh. It's bending ... it's going to break.

Right. Sycamores are wide at the bottom but they thin out, with fewer branches at the top. Not ideal for man or bear to climb.

There's another man and ... is that a bear behind him? Oh my God! It is a bear, and it's after those guys ... It's too close—I can't take a chance and shoot it. Oh no. The branch broke. The big guy crashed on the ground. He's out, but the skinny guy is stuck up in the tree with the bear, and he can't go any higher. The bear's claws are on his leg ... it's got him ... it's chewing ...

He uses a microphone to shout at the bear, hoping to frighten it. José kicks with his other leg, but the bear has tasted blood, and it's not letting go. The pilot revs up the engine, hoping the sound will stop the bear. It doesn't. The bear continues to gnaw on the man's leg. The other man who fell out of the tree also kicks at something. Captain Henderson recognizes it.

"What do you know? It's the same terrier I saw at the waterfall." It darts at the man's ankles, and the man kicks it.

Adolpho, you just don't get it. Kicking doesn't slow YoYo down. It's an opportunity he uses to find a weak spot. Captain Henderson may not see it, but YoYo gets in quite a few good nips. Adolpho only got a single. Score another round for YoYo.

"Arrow Wing to control. Located two men in the woods … in a tree. One fell out, and he's headed back along the shore. Small dog is following him. Same dog sighted earlier … a terrier. The other man is still in the tree. A bear is mauling him. He's in imminent danger, but I can't risk a shot. Advise search teams that getting here is urgent. To save the man's life. Returning to base. Henderson, over and out."

There is nothing the pilot can do for José. Maybe a team will get there in time to save him. Adolpho is easily captured. YoYo's yapping leads the team right to him.

News that the dog has been located spreads fast at the center. Now that the world has heard the story, YoYo is a hero. Holly waits for him, impatiently pacing the shore. At midnight, a squad of National Guardsmen arrives with Adolpho. An exhausted YoYo is tucked in a backpack. Holly picks him up and hugs him, plants kisses on his head, and whispers how happy she is to see him. She notes his mud-caked coat, long tufts of the golden crown falling in his eyes, and lots of scratches all over his body. He licks her nose—in fact, her whole face—and lapses into those *HehHehHeh* sounds. Now we can all go home.

Not all of us go home, though. Hector goes to the hospital to be treated for third-degree burns. Adolpho goes for injuries from the fall, wounds from the bear's claws, and bites on his ankles from we know who. The FBI, the DEA, and ICE line up to question both men. Officers stay on duty to wait for the bus to be raised in the morning. The teams don't find José—only a bloody trail. The bear turns up miles away and is left to wander in the forest. Authorities suspect that José escaped to Mexico. Maybe, but I wouldn't bet that he returned to his old gang, the Sinaloa cartel. Word got back to them that he made a deal with the Zeta cartel to hijack the shipment from Hector. Wherever he is, he will have to watch his back. For the rest of his predictably short life.

Hector and Adolpho are okay with the cartel. They weren't part of the hijack. However, neither of them needs to worry about going back to

Mexico in the near future. They'll spend a lot of time in federal prison. So who won the fight? The decision is coming ... here it is: At least nine rounds for YoYo. Zero for the drug runners. It's official. YoYo is declared the winner. Sounds right to me! In fact, he's sitting on Holly's lap right now, barking, *Yiii–wwwooowww*. No translation is needed. And don't ask me how he knew.

Chapter Twenty-Two

YoYo wanted to play when he got home at 3:00 a.m. He ran straight for the toy box to get a squeaky. Holly cut up broiled chicken—his first meal in almost twenty-four hours, not counting a partially chewed bear toe. He was hungry. Not a bite was left for BoBo to clean up. It's 4:00 a.m., and everyone sleeps peacefully except YoYo, who is snuggled into a down comforter next to Holly. He's having a nightmare, and he kicks and growls in his sleep. Holly gives him a reassuring pat. I rest in my favorite place, perched on the stereo speakers and contemplate my progress with the mission. I'm also thinking about the potential of a reward. I admit I've always been a bit of a gambler. If I make the right wish, there could be lots of possibilities. But for what? What could I wish for that would keep me feeling as though I'm alive? I think I know. The telephone interrupts my meditation—and Holly's sleep—early the next morning.

"Hello."

In the background, Holly hears, "I want my doggie."

"Mrs. Hancock, it's Mac. We have a problem because Chrissie thinks Lucky is hers. I realize this is an imposition, but I wonder if we could bring her over so she can see that Lucky already has a home."

"Captain MacDonald, why don't you just call me Holly? After all we've been through together, I think we can be on a first-name basis, don't you?"

"Well, yes, Holly, if you call me Mac. We don't need the 'Captain' anymore, either."

"Good. If you give me an hour to get organized here, I'll be delighted to have Chrissie visit YoYo. In fact, you can bring her as often as you want. It's good for YoYo too."

"Thank you. Amy and I will bring her over later this morning."

Holly has barely set the phone down when it rings again. It's Katy. "We miss Lucky."

Holly invites the Hansen family to join them for a reunion. The next call comes from the twins' nanny.

"Can we take Lucky home with us? The girls want him so bad."

Holly doesn't want to disappoint them, so they're invited to join the others. Katy calls back to ask whether it's okay to bring Vickie and Willie with them. I can't wait to hear YoYo's reaction to the whole group coming to his house. That is, if they can get by the gaggle of reporters on the front lawn. TV trucks line the streets. Reporters lurk outside the door. Holly isn't up to facing them this early, so BoBo and YoYo don't get their morning walk. Instead they go in the backyard where they can have a little privacy for their routine. But some photographers peek over the wall, and cameras click away.

The routine begins with YoYo. He meticulously sniffs for a spot, preferably conspicuous. He finds an acceptable leaf, and his leg goes up. He squirts. Then he turns back to sniff that leaf, possibly to verify not only that the mission is accomplished, but that it is indeed his squirt. Now BoBo moves in, sniffs the spot, and maneuvers so his stream precisely covers YoYo's. He doesn't need confirmation and continues to follow YoYo around the yard.

If YoYo's squirt was a message, BoBo hit the "delete" key. If it's territorial, BoBo just peed on YoYo's flag. If it's a competition, the loser is the first to run out of ammunition. That race is hard to handicap. BoBo has more, but YoYo is stingy—a pee-pincher. None of the above deters the photographers, and they click till the deeds are done. They'll be great photos—revealing interesting canine behavior.

YoYo gets a special breakfast this morning: New York top sirloin, rare, cut in tiny pieces. There's no favoritism, so BoBo gets his share, although he's already filled up on kibble. But he's a Lab, and Labs never turn down food. Both dogs settle down for a nap on the big, round cushion until the doorbell calls them into action. BoBo runs for a ball, and he greets the visitors with it, ready to play. YoYo barks his usual, standard short *aafff ... aafff ... aaaffff*s while his nose works to identify "friend or foe."

Chrissie cries, "My doggie," and reaches for him. That's too aggressive for YoYo, and he retreats behind Holly.

"Put your hand out, Chrissie, so he can smell it. That will tell him who you are."

Moments later, the two are on the big cushion, cooing at each other. Mac watches in amazement.

"I guess I have to get her a dog of her own. Unless she moves in with you, Holly."

"Or you can just give YoYo to Chrissie," Amy offers. "We'll take good care of him."

They laugh at her joke because they know Holly would never give YoYo up. The doorbell rings again, and Sibel and Mabel walk in like Siamese twins until Mabel runs to hug Chrissie. Sibel heads for YoYo, making him happy when she squeezes the squeakies. Ted leaves the door open, and Katy, Tommy, Scotty, Vickie, and Willie join the party. The door is still open, and a few bold photographers invite themselves in. You can't blame them. They want pictures of this reunion. There is still an enormous appetite to see and hear more of this story. Photos will show loving, joyous children playing with the little dog who saved their lives. What a happy ending for a story that began as a tragedy.

Days later Holly is annoyed that reporters keep calling.

"They all want interviews," she tells Ted. "I'm not going through that again. Have to think of something that will put an end to it even before it starts."

She's ready for the next reporter who stands at the door, recorder in hand.

"We heard rumors about YoYo. That he was used as a secret weapon. Is it true that he was involved in that terrorist attack in the federal building?"

Holly and Ted exchange looks. Laughing, she invites the reporter in and launches her counteroffensive.

"Let me tell you about the real YoYo," she begins.

"I was in the kitchen when he went out into the backyard. Moments later, he ran full bore into the house. Took cover behind the sofa. His ears were back, and he trembled. I coaxed and coaxed, but YoYo would not come out. I realized that something must have frightened him. Something in the backyard. So I went into the garden, fully expecting to see at least a coyote. They've gotten into neighbors' yards and chewed up their dogs.

"Well, guess what? A big surprise waited for me. The object of YoYo's terror was a white possum. About two feet long. Maybe it weighed about fifteen pounds. YoYo probably spotted it digging in the compost pile looking for worms. I'm sure he would have barked at it and charged. I suspect the possum waddled off a short distance. Then it stopped, stood on its hind legs, and hissed with bared teeth. YoYo got the message that this was no rat, and his chase skidded to a halt." Holly pauses to chuckle before continuing her purposeful tale.

"I know because I've had encounters with possums. This is how they react when someone confronts them. They're little fighters. Hisses continued, then segued into loud, high-pitched clicks. I could still hear it scolding in the tree. The mystery was solved.

"So, to answer your question, if anyone thinks YoYo can be used as a weapon, the answer is yes—*if* the enemy is smaller than a possum. Then he can do the job. Although, to be honest, he has yet to catch the lizard he hunts every day."

Ted winks at Holly. She did it. The reporters didn't uncover any secret weapon and have to be satisfied watching YoYo race around the room with one of his toys. Even so, he's a candidate for exploitation, so here's my prediction: YoYo's a hero ... kids love him and start using his name. "It's YoYo" means "It's supercool." His picture will show up on cereal boxes and T-shirts. Maybe there will even be a Demon Dog comic book.

Here are more predictions. Well, maybe a little more than predictions—I confess to finding a back door. After a month, the paparazzi will disappear, but still the calls and letters will keep coming. Holly can't take BoBo and YoYo for a walk in the park without an endless parade of children and well-wishers following. The phone keeps ringing and people, strangers, drop in constantly to see YoYo. It increases until one day Ted makes an announcement: "I want to live a normal life. I've had enough of this celebrity stuff."

Ted and Holly are writers, so they can live anywhere and continue working. After a long discussion, they rent their house out for a year and move to France. I wish I could forecast a happy future for them in that small apartment in Paris, which allows dogs. The French are quite dog-tolerant. In fact, if you want good service in a restaurant, take your dog. It ensures a lot of attention, even from the kitchen. Chefs are only too happy to send out a plate for Fido. But that vision clouds up the first time Holly takes the dogs for a walk. Minutes later, she rushes back. She's upset.

"Ted," she says, "don't unpack. We can't stay here. By the time I walked half a block, ten people stopped me. 'C'est YoYo? YoYo c'est un beau chien. YoYoYoYo—can I pet YoYo? Can I bring my children to see YoYo?' Ted, it's the same here. We've got to find another place."

They try New Zealand, but Facebook and Twitter have preceded them. The citizens immediately recognize YoYo and become enamored of him. Half the country wants to "drop by" and pet him. Next, they fly to Japan, where the people are polite and considerate—normally. But YoYo inspires adulation, and millions of cameras lie in wait for him. They escape to a sparsely populated island in the South Pacific where he is admired, but not for his heroism or his monumental breakthrough with speech. What impresses the natives is a signal he developed. It's a high-pitched bark with a 1-2-2 beat—*rrrrfff … rrrrfff … rrrrfff … rrrfff … fffff.* He only does it when a Komodo dragon is in the neighborhood. Fortunately, he knows better than to chase it like the lizard at home. He has to be contented with the game he plays with crabs on the beach.

For the children, I have one final prediction: This is more than a happy ending. It's also a new beginning for them. When they were thrust into that wild and dangerous adventure, they couldn't have dreamed how many wonderful, exciting opportunities it would bring. How it would affect their lives. New beginnings always do. I can attest to that. Which reminds me—I got a message: "Angela, it's time to come home."

I've been recalled. I don't want to go. I don't want this mission to end. But I have no choice. I will return to the Dimension and submit the final report to the Committee. It will show how YoYo fought, attacked, and defended, and in every instance he used the same tool. His bark. But different barks for different situations. Can there be any doubt that these were messages? When we study that noisy mixture of vowels and consonants, I know we'll find more words. Yes, words. In English. Proof that evolution has done its job.

I wish I could tell humans that if they want to understand what the Fidos of the world are saying, they must pay more attention to those barks. They must make an effort to translate them into words. The benefits would be considerable. For instance, translations could open the floodgates of love and loyalty that the dog offers. Human development would advance. Loneliness would disappear. It would be a better world. The Committee patiently waits for this enlightenment. It has been a noble mission because YoYo has given us hope. He already makes us laugh at his antics. I wouldn't be surprised if someday he told a joke.

In time, perhaps a few hundred years, another mission will be sent to check the progress that dogs have made with speech. Another dog will be selected. And another angel. Why? Because, regardless of where they came from originally, all spirits in the Dimension have an unbounded love for *Canis familiaris*. They are astonished that Earth was the lucky recipient of such incredible beings.

Another message just arrived. "Angela, the mission was successful. You may choose your reward."

Reward? I keep forgetting about that. Now I have to decide. Do I want to move up a level or be granted a single wish? I'm thinking that if I move up, I'll just be another level away from YoYo. Not to mention further from alive. So here's my decision.

To the Committee: In closing, I say "Thank you" for sending me on this mission. I feel that "Thank you" is inadequate to express my gratitude for the extended time with my beloved YoYo. It was so precious to me ... I find that it's beyond my ability to express myself in words. So I will revert to our language—^^^^^{{{{{ --+++/*

And, with your permission, I have made a decision—on what to ask for as my reward.

I decline to move up to a new level, although I am certain it would be sublime, and I would be in the most superior company. Instead, I opt to make a wish. What I have selected as my reward may be looked upon with disfavor. It may be selfish or self-serving. But, strangely enough, I believe that at last I have found my voice—the one I never had before. A calling, perhaps limited, but something I totally love.

My wish is to be sent on another mission. One that would give me an opportunity to make a contribution. All my life, I wanted to be helpful. A new mission could be that opportunity. I know that it could take me to strange and unknown places. With it, though, is the possibility of exciting adventures. After a new mission, I can return to the Dimension to wait for my beloved YoYo.

Respectfully,

}{>^<

The answer comes quickly. My wish is approved. I will be given another mission. Now it's time to say good-bye to YoYo. It's probably a good time because he's asleep on his little blue blanket that says, "Yorkies Forever."

I don't know how I can leave him. From the moment I arrived, we've been inseparable. But I know I can't stay. One last time, I'll get as close to him as possible. I move to the blue blanket where I can look into that sweet face. I won't see it anymore. Already I miss him so much it hurts. I want to rustle through his soft fur, encircle his little body to say good-bye, but it might upset him.

That's silly of me. He doesn't even know I'm here, so how can my leaving affect him? It can't, and I'm indulging in wishful thinking. I use the only option I have—I envelop him in my space. A substitute for a hug.

Oh, he's stirred. He looks into my space. He tilts his head and makes a sound. As if he's trying to say something. His jaws move, and his teeth click together. It sounds like an *s*. It *is* an S! At last he has managed the difficult *s*! His jaw drops open. Out comes an *aaarrrr*. He pauses to release an *ooohhhrrr*. That's three syllables. Another pause, and his tongue clicks on the roof of his mouth. It's unbelievable, but that was an *n*, followed by another *arrrr*. His head goes back, and there's an *aaaahhh*. It's a word. A word with four syllables.

Now there's a different sound. A hiccup. Or is it a hiccup? He does it again. I pay close attention. This is important. But what is it? His tail is tucked under, and his ears are back against his head. His lips curve down and tremble. He does it again and again. What is it? Oh, oh, oh. No. It can't be. The sound is coming from his nose and his throat. He's using both systems. That's what humans do when they cry. What's going on? Could he …? Yes. YoYo is crying. What should I do?

Wide eyes look directly into my space. He wags his tail—to the right. We stare at each other—I look into his eyes—he into my space. He knows! I grip him tighter in the envelope. We stay together for a long time. Finally, the realization comes. I can leave now. And with me, I take his last word.

"Sayonara."

Farewell, sweet YoYo, till we meet again.

The End

About the Author

Lori Hamilton has enjoyed several varied careers that include acting on the stage and TV, lecturing, doing seminars for UCLA's extension, and producing and writing highly rated television documentaries. A big switch occurred when she began designing women's apparel. That resulted in not just designing, but manufacturing the line that was sold in major stores throughout the country. Ultimately, she opted out from that career to become a farmer in Ventura County. Currently she does programs for the Los Angeles Unified School District to instruct children on the benefits of eating fresh vegetables and fruit.

Through all this, there has been one constant. She was never without her beloved dogs. So many breeds … German shepherds, a Border collie, a poodle, even a Tennessee black-and-tan coonhound. The last addition was a Yorkie, YoYo, who was the inspiration for *Demon Dog*. Now Lori is content to stay home in Camarillo, California, with her husband and write novels while YoYo and BoBo, a black lab, keep her company.

CPSIA information can be obtained at www.ICGtesting.com
Printed in the USA
LVOW05s1959210114

370389LV00004B/18/P

9 781491 702628